OTHER TEAM REAPER THRILLERS

RETRIBUTION
DEADLY INTENT
TERMINATION ORDER
BLOOD RUSH
KILL COUNT
RELENTLESS
LETHAL TENDER

EMPTY QUIVER

A TEAM REAPER THRILLER

BRENT TOWNS

WOLFPACK PUBLISHING
— EST 2013 —

WOLFPACK
PUBLISHING
— EST 2013 —

Published in the United States by Wolfpack Publishing, Las Vegas

Wolfpack Publishing
6032 Wheat Penny Avenue
Las Vegas, NV 89122

wolfpackpublishing.com

Paperback ISBN 978-1-64119-856-1
eBook ISBN 978-1-64119-855-4

Library of Congress Control Number: 2019951426

EMPTY QUIVER

"I am not afraid of an army of lions led by a sheep; I am afraid of an army of sheep led by a lion."

Alexander the Great

Empty Quiver: *Refers to the seizure, theft, or loss of a functioning nuclear weapon –Wikipedia.*

From the Central Intelligence Agency World Fact Book:

Kashmir: *The site of the world's largest and most militarized territorial dispute.*

India: *World's largest producer of licit opium for the pharmaceutical trade. But an undetermined quantity is diverted to the world's illicit markets.*

Pakistan: *Significant transit area for Afghan drugs, including heroin, opium, morphine, and hashish.*
    Both India and Pakistan are nuclear powers.

CHAPTER ONE

Zabul Province, Afghanistan

"Talk to me, Reaper," Cara's even voice filled his head, coming through the ear-piece of his comms unit.

Six-foot-four, John 'Reaper' Kane, solidly built with black hair, currently with thick stubble on his tanned face, felt a rivulet of sweat trickle down his nose and fall through space, splashing onto the fine dust between his feet.

More of the salty water created a runnel down his muscular back, leaving a glistening trail over the Reaper tattoo that gave the ex-recon marine his name. His outstretched right hand was rock-steady with a Sig Sauer M17 handgun pointed across the cramped and stuffy room with almost impenetrable mud-brick walls.

"Reaper, you copy?" The voice was more insistent.

Kane depressed the talk button on his comms and

said, "I'm a bit busy at the moment, Reaper Two."

"Just so you know, our HVT is getting away in a white SUV. If we don't move now, we'll lose him."

Cara Billings, callsign Reaper Two and the team's sniper, was on overwatch while the rest of Team Reaper infiltrated the Zabul Province green zone.

"Deal with it."

"You're not coming?"

"No."

"What about Axe?"

"He's busy too," Kane said, glancing down briefly at the thick beard of the prone figure in the deep hole at his feet, before returning his gaze to the job at hand.

"Copy that. Out."

"Now," sighed Kane. "Where were we?"

"You die, infidel," sneered a thick-bearded Afghan insurgent, a thin bead of sweat on his brow, caused by a combination the heat and the tense anxiety of the situation. His eyes flicked about nervously but returned to center on Kane.

"Just hold on a moment, Ahab, before you go and clack off that suicide vest you're wearing. Maybe we can discuss this calmly, and perhaps all of us can walk away alive."

"My name is not Ahab," the Afghani hissed. "It is Aarash."

"Close. I never was much good with my pronunciation."

Kane's team had come into Zabul Province after Fahim Noor. Leader of the local insurgent population and owner of the majority of vast poppy fields which provided the funds for all his activities, both at home and abroad.

The compound had been breached by Kane and his team, sans Cara, who was presently two-hundred meters outside the green zone on the slope of a steep hill, the crosshairs of her scope on the white SUV containing their high-value target.

On entry, Brick and Arenas had swept left while Kane and Axe went in the opposite direction. Which had brought them to their current position; facing an Afghani suicide bomber with his thumb on the trigger, while Axe took a nap in the hole they'd found in the floor of the room.

Kane couldn't be certain whether his friend was even alive. He knew the big ex-recon marine sniper had taken a round; he just wasn't sure where.

"Ahab –"

"Aarash!" came the shouted response of the sweating man.

Kane nodded. He could tell the man didn't want to die. He could almost smell the fear emanating from every pore of the darkened skin. The Team Reaper commander nodded. "Aarash. You don't want to die, just like me, yeah?"

"I would die in a heartbeat for the Prophet."

"And you will if you take your finger off that

8 BRENT TOWNS

fucking button. Think about it. Do you have a family, Aarash?"

"What about them?"

"Who will take care of them after you are gone?"

Aarash glanced at a closed door to his left. "They will join me in Paradise."

Son of a bitch, the crazy bastar♦'s family were in the next room. "You want to kill them too?"

"If it is Allah's will."

"Reaper One? Zero. Copy?"

The inquiry from Kane's immediate superior Luis Ferrero, who also commanded the Bravo element of the Worldwide Drug Initiative, went unanswered. A few heartbeats later, he came back again. "Reaper One? Zero. Copy?"

Once again Kane pressed the talk button on his comms without taking his eyes from the man before him. "Can't talk right now, Zero. Trying to defuse a situation."

"What kind of situation, Reaper?"

"The kind that goes boom."

"Do you need assistance, Reaper One?" another voice chimed in.

"Negative, ma'am," Kane said to General Mary Thurston. "Assistance won't help this time."

"Copy. Good luck."

"I am through talking to you, infidel," Aarash snarled vehemently, removing his thumb from the red trigger button.

———————

The muscular flesh of Cara's shoulder bore the full force of the CheyTac Intervention .408 sniper rifle's recoiling butt. The projectile set out at around eleven hundred meters per second to slam through the side window of the SUV, shattering the glass and punching a hole in the driver's head.

Lacking human control, the vehicle swung savagely to the right and tipped, the impetus forcing it along in a skid until friction robbed it of its motion, bringing it to a grinding halt on its side.

"Reaper Three, Reaper Five, target vehicle down east of the compound. You need to get to it now."

"Copy, Reaper Two. We're on our way."

Cara Billings was in her mid-thirties, with short dark hair and a tough, slim build. Besides being second in command to Kane, she was also the team's armorer.

She studied the wrecked SUV through her scope but saw no movement. Cara took a moment to scan the immediate surrounds, noting that there was nothing that looked to be out of place.

Suddenly her comms crackled to life. "Reaper Two? Bravo Three. Copy?"

"Copy, Bravo Three."

Bravo Three was Master Sergeant Pete Teller. He was USAF and the second seat at the UAV console. His pilot was Brooke Reynolds, ex-DEA, who flew under the callsign Bravo One.

"Reaper Two, there are two technicals approaching from the south. Both look to have fifty caliber weapons mounted on the back."

"Copy that, Bravo Three," Cara acknowledged and shifted her scope to locate the approaching vehicles.

Both were white with dark patches, which on closer inspection appeared to be decals. Large dust plumes shot out from their rear wheels and billowed into the clear blue sky, leaving a dirty smudge in their wake. There looked to be two men in the front with an additional pair in the rear. But with two fifty cals, it would make all the difference.

"Reaper Three, where are you guys?" Cara asked.

An explosion of red appeared from between a couple of trees as a beat-up vehicle advanced from behind the green screen. Cara's comms crackled to life and Brick's voice cut through the howl of background noise, "We're almost there. Don't shoot the guys in the red Mustang."

Cara breathed out an exasperated sigh. "Shit. You guys are both crazy."

"What better way to go into battle than to ride a beautiful horse such as this?"

"Tell that to the Indians who are behind you, General Custer."

It was at that point that two things happened. The first was the eruption of noise and lead from the two fifty caliber machine guns that opened fire. The second was an explosion which rocked the center of the compound.

A fifty caliber round punched through the Mustang's rear window before burning through the interior of the vehicle, blowing out the front windscreen in a spray of glass that resembled confetti at a wedding. The blast of wind caused by the Mustang's forward motion was immediate.

"Shit! Fuck!" Richard 'Brick' Peters cried out as he witnessed the fragmentation and disappearance of the windscreen. The Team Reaper combat medic brought up his Heckler & Koch 416 and turned as best he could in his seat to let loose with a sustained burst of automatic fire.

Through the shattered back window, the big ex-SEAL with the shaved head and tattooed arms saw geysers erupt from the dirt road behind them. He watched in horror as they stitched a path to the rear of the Mustang and then punched into the rear of the vehicle.

"Carlos, turn right!"

Carlos Arenas, AKA Reaper Three, swung hard on the wheel, flicking the rear end of the Mustang out in a long slide, then gave it some gas and it straightened up. The former Mexican Special Forces commander had immediate control of the vehicle.

"What is it, Amigo?"

Brick looked at one of the smoking fist-sized holes in the back of the vehicle as he took a fresh magazine from his tactical vest. He slapped it home and said, "We have a hole as big as my dick in the back of this thing."

"They must be using a small-caliber weapon then, my friend," Arenas smirked. "We are safe."

"Yeah, whatever," Brick said, firing another burst from his 416.

The Mustang hit a bump in the road, and his head hit the roof. "Son of a bitch, Carlos, can't you drive any better?"

"I can stop if you would like?"

"Bravo Three, we need some help with these bastards, if you don't mind," Brick said into his comms.

"Copy, Reaper Five. Give me a moment, and I'll see what I can do."

Back in the ops center in Kandahar, fingers flashed across a keyboard as Teller readied the MQ-1 Predator which was overhead at ten thousand feet. Beside him, Brooke Reynolds awaited his OK to fire.

Moments passed before his voice crackled over the comms and Brick heard him say, "Reaper Five, you have a Hellfire inbound. Don't forget to duck."

"Copy that."

The AGM-114 Hellfire missile streaked across the sky at Mach 1.3 and closed the distance between the UAV and its target in virtually no time at all.

A fireball erupted from behind the Mustang as the rocket-propelled lance exploded, destroying the lead technical.

The one behind it swerved violently to the right to avoid crashing into its frontrunner. It skidded sideways before the driver showed some skill behind the wheel and straightened before it tipped over.

The gunner hung on for dear life before gathering himself. Baring his yellow teeth, he opened fire once more with the machine gun, determined to kill the two Team Reaper operators. The heavy-caliber bullets seemed to tear the Mustang apart, with both Arenas and Brick feeling the passage of each shot, and would later reminisce about how they'd felt about coming so close to meeting their maker, and how lucky they were to be alive.

"I think it is time we leave, my friend," Arenas shouted across at Brick.

"I'm with you, Amigo."

They threw their doors wide and seemed to roll out of the fast-moving Mustang with all the grace of a rock. Both men hit hard and rolled several times before sliding to a stop on the dirt road.

They came up onto their knees and reached for their M17s, having lost their carbines in the violent evacuation of the doomed vehicle.

Behind the operators the red machine suddenly exploded into flame, the orange fireball reaching up into the hot Afghan sky, raining down twisted pieces of metal in their vicinity.

The last SUV came hurtling toward them. A bump in the road was hit at speed, causing it to leap like a graceful gazelle, then gravity forcing it down with a crash. Arenas and Brick opened fire with their sidearms.

Within moments, both men had blown through half of their seventeen shot magazines. The front windscreen of the oncoming vehicle shattered under the impact of the lead barrage, but it kept on. Then the SUV ran over a pressure plate buried beneath the road's surface.

The blast blew the battered SUV, engulfed in flames, skyward. As the vehicle rose, the shooter holding the fifty-caliber gun was on fire, and the sight of the flaming man seemed too surreal.

As it crashed back down, bits of burning metal, glass, and liquid scattered across the road. Brick glanced at Arenas and said, "Sure glad that wasn't us who hit the IED."

The Mexican nodded. "Would have been a bad end to a shitty day."

"Reaper Three, are you guys OK?"

"Yes, ma'am," Arenas replied to Cara's inquiry. "Never been better."

"Good. Check the target vehicle. I have to go. I think that first bang was Reaper getting blown up."

———————

Kane couldn't hear shit except for the high-pitched ringing in his ears. He spat dirt and grit from his mouth and tried to see through the heavy dust haze which had enveloped him. His comms crackled in his ear. He coughed and managed to get out, "Reaper Two, copy?"

Static.

"Reaper Two, copy?"

Still nothing.

Kane tried to move, but the motion caused his muscles to scream in protest. His hands touched something soft, and a gruff voice said, "Get your hand out of my fucking face."

"Axe?"

"Are we still alive, Reaper?" his friend growled.

"Just barely. I can feel blood running down my face."

"Stop shouting."

"What?'

"Get off me!"

Recall of the situation hit Kane like a train. He remembered the Afghani with the vest, the compound, Axe getting shot, and the hole in the floor he'd dived into when he realized what the man was about to do. *Axe!*

"Axe, you're alive!"

"Won't be for much longer. Get off me and stop shouting."

The two men managed to dig their way out of the debris that had fallen on them and pulled themselves out of the hole, but the dust was still so thick that they couldn't see. "Axe, are your comms working? Try Cara."

"Reaper Two, copy?"

The question remained unanswered.

"Reaper Two, copy?"

Suddenly, light filtered through the dust and a voice called out, "Stop your shouting and get your sorry asses out here."

They made their way over and through the rubble of the damaged building until they were both out in the sunshine, covered in layers of dust. Kane's face had an extra thick wad of crusted dirt where dust had adhered and mixed with a smear of blood.

"What happened?" Cara asked them.

"Some guy wanted to meet his maker and clacked off an explosive vest. That was after he shot Axe."

Concern was etched on Cara's face. "Are you OK?"

"Got my vest. I fell into a hole in the floor, hit my head and got knocked out."

"What's happening?" Kane asked loudly, his hearing not back to normal yet.

"Wait for a moment, and I'll find out," Cara said and then into her comms, "Reaper Three, copy?"

"Copy."

"What's the status of our HVT? Over."

There was a moment of hesitation, and then the

Mexican's accented voice replied, "We may have a little problem."

———————

"I can't fucking believe this shit," Brick cursed. "Will you just shoot the prick?"

Arenas' M17 was held in an unwavering fist, pointed at their HVT, who was holding a Glock to the side of the ex-SEAL's bald head. "Just shut up and stop moving," the Mexican grunted.

"I ain't the one moving, damn it!"

The situation was almost comical. Events leading up to that point in time had unfolded like a bad movie. When they had approached the crashed SUV that contained their target, they'd been searching for him, before he'd appeared behind them and now held his gun to Brick's head.

There was blood running from a gash above Noor's right eye, where he'd hit his head during the crash. His mouth was curled up into a vicious snarl, and for the third time, he barked, "Put your weapon down, or I will kill your friend!"

Arenas shrugged. "He is not my friend."

"Aww, hell no. You did not just say that."

"You wish for me to lie?"

"Fine time to tell a man you don't like him, just when he's about to die."

Arenas shrugged. "My conscience is clear."

"Great. Well, fuck you too."

The gun in the Mexican's hand fired, and Noor's head snapped back as the slug from the M17 blew his brains out of the back of his head. He dropped like a stone; eyes wide with shock.

Brick stared hard at Arenas and said, "I am your friend, right?"

The Mexican shook his head. "You are welcome."

"You are, right?"

Arenas said into his comms, "Zero? Reaper Three. HVT is down. I say again, HVT is down."

"Copy, Reaper Three. The target is down. Search the compound for intel and then move to extract."

"Roger that. Reaper One, did you get that?"

The answer came from Cara, not Kane. "Copy, Reaper Three. Search the SUV and then move to us, over."

"Copy. Reaper Three, out."

A secure facility outside of Lahore, Pakistan

Captain Deepak Habib's blood ran cold. His eyes began to bulge, and his pulse quickened. "This can't be right," he muttered to himself.

He went back to the start and began to count again. This time he was sure to be more careful how he went about it.

The same number as last time. He licked his lips

nervously and went back to start again. Since 1972 Pakistan had been developing nuclear weapons. Finally, in 1998, in response to India conducting its second nuclear test, Pakistan detonated five nuclear devices, after which it created its own stockpile of weapons. The total of their recorded stockpile was ninety-eight.

As he neared the end of his count for the third time, a sense of dread overwhelmed him when he realized that he was coming up short. The result, this time, was exactly the same as the first two. Ninety-six.

It would appear that Pakistan was missing two devices. Full of fear, the man ran for the nearest phone.

National Security Agency, Fort Meade, Maryland

Scott Bald careened along the hallway towards his boss' office, almost knocking over one of the senior analysts as he went, a partially crumpled piece of paper in his hand.

"Why don't you watch where you're going?" the man growled after the fast-moving man.

"Sorry, sir," Bald called back over his shoulder as he put on another burst of speed.

When he reached the office, he threw the door open, the wooden object crashing back against its stopper as the man hurried in. From behind his desk, Kent Miller looked up with more than passing annoyance on his face. "What the hell?!"

The analyst thrust the piece of paper under Miller's nose. "I'm sorry, sir, but we've got an Empty Quiver."

"What the...? You're shitting me?" Miller said as he grabbed the sheet from before his face.

"No, sir, this call was intercepted no more than ten minutes ago. The caller was a captain in the Pakistan army who works at a secure facility where nuclear warheads have been stockpiled."

"Obviously it isn't too fucking secure, is it?"

"No, sir."

"The Whitehouse is going to go ballistic," Miller snapped.

Bald winced. "Yes, sir."

"Leave it with me, Scott. This isn't going to be pretty."

Within thirty minutes, all the top agency directors were assembled in the Whitehouse situation room for an emergency meeting. Word went out across the globe to all their respective agents. They were to find Pakistan's lost nukes, no matter what.

Pakistan-Azad Kashmir Border

Just short of the border checkpoint, an unmarked truck ground to a halt. Like its canvas covering, the cab was a khaki-green color. Inside the cabin, seated beside his driver, Colonel Ajeet Khan watched the guard approach the vehicle.

Before speaking, the soldier snapped a salute to the officer. "Your papers please, Colonel."

Dark eyes stared at the soldier before he passed the appropriate documents to him. The guard checked the validity of the papers and nodded before handing them back. "I will need to check the back."

Khan nodded brusquely and waved the man away.

The guard saluted once more, but instead of going about his business, he frowned with his gaze directed at Khan's chest or the ribbons which decorated the colonel's uniform to be exact. "You wear the Nishan-e-Haider, Colonel?"

The Nishan-e-Haider, which translated to the Emblem of the Lion, was the highest medal of valor awarded in the Pakistan armed forces. However, to qualify, you had to commit an act of bravery and be killed doing it.

Khan looked down at the green ribbon and then back up at the border guard. He fingered his black mustache nonchalantly and shrugged his shoulders. "I am sorry," he said sincerely.

Confused by the words, the guard opened his

mouth to speak when a bullet from the colonel's SIG P226 smashed through the roof of it and up into his brain.

The crack of the shot alerted four soldiers from the Pakistan Army Special Service Group or as they were known, the Maroon Berets. Each man was armed with an MP5SD. It was the suppressed variant of the standard MP5 used by the special forces community.

From the small, square guard post, an additional three border guards appeared. All were armed with AK-47s and fumbled to get their weapons up and firing. It was painful to watch as the highly trained special forces soldiers cut them down in a matter of heartbeats. Bodies jerked as the bullets hammered home with deadly efficiency.

When the gunfire ceased, Khan climbed from the truck, his P226 still in his hand. He walked around each of the fallen border guards individually and shot them in the head.

When he was done, he turned to his most trusted man, Havildar, or Sergeant Feroz Bawa, a big thickset man with dark skin. "Get the bodies off the road. I want to be at the old hydropower plant before dark."

"Yes, sir."

The men set about dragging the corpses into the small guard hut. Once they were done, Khan said to Bawa, "Once we arrive and the warheads are unloaded, you will leave for India to get the package. Take twenty men with you. We must have the package if we are to succeed in our mission."

Bawa nodded. He had served with Khan for the past five years, each man having fought in different parts of the world, including Kashmir. However, for what they needed to accomplish in this mission, Kashmir was the perfect place to do it.

They all climbed back onto the truck, and the driver turned the engine over. The truck roared to life with a puff of black diesel smoke. The driver shifted the stick and with a loud crunch, jammed it into gear. When he let out the clutch, they were moving once more.

CHAPTER TWO

Kandahar, Afghanistan

As the Black Hawk came in to land, General Mary Thurston stood watching as it set down on the concrete pad. An athletically built woman in her early forties, the general had long dark hair pulled back in a severe bun. Behind her aviator sunglasses were brown eyes that rarely missed anything when it came to observing things on the ground, and her stance spoke of a confident person who'd served her country in both war and peace. BDU pants clad her muscular legs, and a khaki T-shirt hugged her torso, accentuating her curves.

She watched on as her team disembarked from the helo. Kane and Axe still carried their coating of dust, while Arenas and Brick appeared to be a little worse for wear. Cara, however, looked to be the only one among them that seemed OK.

Luis Ferrero stepped up beside Thurston and shook his head. "It seems like every time we send the children out to play, they come back filthy or with skin off."

She glanced at the ex-DEA agent, his hair graying. "What else do you expect with parents like us?"

Ferrero chuckled and said, "Speak for yourself."

The team gathered in front of them and stood wearily. "Well, look at you," Thurston said. "You come home with the ass out of your pants, beat up, and the HVT dead as a dodo."

Axe's response was, "I have to protest, ma'am, on the grounds I got shot."

Kane nodded. "Yeah, I got blown up too."

"You're alive, so that's no excuse," the general growled.

"Besides, ma'am, it wasn't us who killed him."

As one, the group turned to look at Arenas. The Mexican toed the ground with a boot then said, "In my defense, I was trying to shoot Brick, but he moved, and the bullet hit Noor in the head by accident."

Kane chuckled which drew a glare from Thurston. "It's not funny. That man would have given us a whole network of drug lines from Afghanistan to the western world. What intel, if any, did you get?"

Kane held up the bag he was carrying. "There's a laptop in there and some papers."

"Give it to Slick when we get back. Get your shit cleaned up and be ready for a briefing in an hour. That's all."

Thurston turned away and walked toward a waiting Humvee. Once she was out of earshot, Kane said, "Mama ain't too happy, Luis."

"She was right. We could have gained a lot of intel from Noor."

Cara looked at her friends and said, "Who's for a beer?"

"Now that is someone who speaks my language," Brick said.

"Beer will have to wait. Briefing first," Ferrero muttered.

"What's going on?" Kane asked.

Ferrero smiled. "You'll find out."

———

Doctor Rosanna Morales dabbed antiseptic on the last of Kane's cuts and said, "That is you done. You can put your shirt on now."

He climbed down from the exam table, the muscles in his back, making the Reaper tattoo on his back seemingly come to life. "Thanks, Doc."

"You boys always seem to get banged up every time you go out."

"It's a rough job."

"Why can't you be more like Cara and try to remain in one piece?"

Cara was standing off to one side, watching the woman work on the others. The doctor was in her early thirties with long brown hair. Until recently, she'd worked as a surgeon in Mexico, but events had led her to become the team's doctor and surgeon.

Kane said, "That's because Cara lays about a lot on missions."

"Someone has to cover your asses. You ready for this briefing now?"

"Lead the way," Kane said. "And thanks, Doc."

"Try to stay out of trouble."

"Maybe."

Kane followed Cara along to the briefing room where the others were gathered, waiting for their arrival. Bravo element was included in the briefing too; Brooke Reynolds, the UAV pilot with long black hair and a tall, athletic build, and Pete Traynor. Traynor, who had worked with Ferrero in the past, before coming with him when the team was formed, was a tall, broad-shouldered man with tattoos and a close-cropped beard courtesy of his undercover work.

Pete Teller was there too as was Sam 'Slick' Swift, the team's computer tech with red hair.

Kane and Cara found a couple of empty chairs and sat down quickly to allow Thurston to begin, "Now that you're all here, we can get started. First off, I've been ordered to fly to India where I'm briefing some high-ranking Indian officers on what we do. The good news is, I get to take two of you along with me as personal protection. Any volunteers?"

No one moved.

"Fantastic. Thanks, Reaper and Traynor. Your willingness to prioritize and participate in my personal safety has warmed my heart."

Cara heard Kane give a low curse. So, apparently, did Thurston. "What was that, Reaper?"

"Just moved the wrong way, ma'am."

"Thought so. Anyway, the rest of you have been assigned an alternative mission. There's a shipment of opium headed through the mountains into Pakistan. Cara will lead the team while Luis will oversee the op from here."

"How are they shipping it, ma'am?" Cara asked.

"Horses. The terrain being traversed is far too rugged for vehicles. You will be provided with maps and aerial surveillance pictures once this briefing is over."

"Yes, ma'am. Is the intel good?"

"As good as can be expected. A CH-47 will airlift you in, and you'll march to an ambush site where you'll set up. The aim of the mission is to stop the drugs from getting over the border."

"Any intel on enemy numbers?" Axe asked.

"Negative."

"UAV, ma'am?" Cara asked.

"Brooke?" Thurston said, looking at Reynolds.

The UAV pilot nodded. "We'll have one up. It'll be fully armed."

"Thank you."

"There is one more thing," Thurston said. "There is a village perhaps two klicks from your insertion point. We're reasonably certain that the Taliban are using it."

Swift cleared his throat. "If they are, ma'am, there's a few of them."

"How many is a few?"

"Maybe thirty."

A pall of silence hung over the briefing room.

Thurston swiftly broke it when she said, "You will all need full body armor and extra ammunition."

"Will we have QRF?" Cara asked. "Since we're going to be hip deep in shit, it might be a good thing to have some backup."

Ferrero walked over to a map on the wall and tapped it with a finger. He said, "This is FOB Johnson. DEA has a FAST team there we can call on if required."

FAST stood for Foreign-deployed and Support Teams. They were in-country operating with Special Operations Forces and the Afghan Army to thwart the Taliban's Opium trade, which was the source of most of their revenue.

"When do we go?"

"Midnight."

"Shit, that soon? But we only just got back."

"I know, but this needs to be done."

"What about the FAST team?"

"They only just got back too."

"Where are we going when this is done?" Cara asked.

"Home to Texas. We'll wait here in country until the general is done in India and then we'll all fly home together."

"All right then."

"Now that's settled let's nut out the details," Thurston said and went back to the start.

———————

Crown Ramada Hotel
Jaipur, India

"Looks like Uncle Sam went all out on this trip, General. No expenses spared," Kane observed as he studied the hotel before them.

"It wasn't Uncle Sam. We're here as guests of the Indian Government."

The hotel before them was built from large sandstone blocks and was adorned with intricate hand-carved works which fascinated the eye. Yellow lights illuminated the front façade, contributing to and highlighting the building's grandeur.

If they thought the exterior of the hotel was awe-inspiring, the interior of the magnificent edifice was doubly so. The floor at the entrance consisted of polished white marble which gave way to red carpet. Spectacularly ornate chandeliers hung from the high ceiling, dousing the foyer with a soft light. Large leafy plants were placed strategically throughout, and in the far corner near the elevators, a stunning waterfall made from natural rock and plants provided a muted but relaxing sound.

As they approached the highly polished mahogany counter, a customer turned away and absent-mindedly ran into Kane. Looking up into the face of the tall American, he gave him a hard stare as though it had been entirely Kane's fault. He then stepped around him and continued to make his way toward the elevators.

"Made a new friend there, Reaper," Traynor said, having observed the man's expression.

"So it would seem," Kane said, glancing back in the man's direction.

After Thurston had checked them in, the porter, having been refused to carry their meager luggage, showed them to their respective rooms on the sixth floor. Kane was impressed with the size and grandeur of his as he looked around, taking it all in. Apart from the ornately carved posts on the dark wood four-poster bed, the walls were covered with a light-colored wallpaper with gold pattern, and a dark wooden ceiling fan with large blades performed lazy circles, stirring the air in the room. The soft furnishings were luxurious, and there was a bowl of fresh fruit and a vase of fresh-cut flowers. Large windows opened out onto a wide balcony, and the fully tiled bathroom had gold taps and towel rails.

He whistled softly to himself and wondered

how much the tab would be if he were picking it up himself. Kane checked his watch when he felt his stomach rumble, and he selected a banana from the fruit bowl. It was nine o'clock.

A soft knock on the door brought Kane swiftly across the room as he hurried to the door. He opened it and found Thurston standing there. "You hungry?"

"And then some," Kane acknowledged. "Was about to eat this." He held up the banana.

"We'll grab Pete and head downstairs to get some chow. How's your room?"

He gave her a wry smile. "I'm almost too scared to touch stuff."

Thurston nodded. "Me too. It isn't like living in the service."

"No, Ma'am, it sure ain't."

CHAPTER THREE

Aboard CH-47, Chicken Hawk One

After being in the air for almost forty minutes, the fumes from the aviation fuel were starting to become too much for those inside the cargo bay of the helicopter. Cara felt like throwing up and thought that the others must be feeling the same. The Loadmaster had just signaled one minute, and she sensed the helicopter start its descent.

With a lurch, she felt the CH-47 touch down, and the ramp traveled the rest of the way to the hardpacked earth of the valley floor.

Through the green hue of her NVGs, the terrain was impossible to make out for the mass of swirling dust being swept up by the rotors of the helicopter. In her comms, she heard the pilot say, "Passengers clear, Chicken Hawk One coming out."

The heavy WHOP-WHOP of the blades slowly

receded into the darkness as the pall of dust finally settled about the team. Cara could finally make out the steep sides of the mountains to her left and right as she scanned their surroundings. She pressed her talk button and said into the mic, "Team sitrep?"

"Three OK."

"Four OK."

"Five OK."

"Two OK," she finished off and then, "Zero? Reaper Two. Radio check, over."

The radio crackled to life. "Copy, Reaper Two. Your signal strength is weak and distorted."

"Damn it," Cara cursed as she looked around. Then, "Carlos, get up that slope to our left and see if you can get a better signal for our comms."

"Yes, ma'am."

While he was gone, she took out her map and had the others gather around. The night was cold and clear, and she felt a chill working its way down her back. Her small red light illuminated the map, and she said, "So, this is where we are, and the Taliban village is back this way two klicks. They will have heard the helo, which means we need to get over this ridge as soon as we can. They won't be able to find any sign until daylight. By then the pack train with the opium should be in sight. Axe, you'll set up your OP just below the crest. If they start coming up after us, don't engage unless I clear it. You will have authorization to call in a UAV strike if required."

"Yes, ma'am."

"All right then," she said, folding the map up and putting it in a pouch. Movement beside them indicated the return of Arenas.

"It is all good. The higher up we go, the better the comms are."

"OK. Let's get over that ridge then."

———————

Afghanistan-Pakistan Border

"Reaper Two, hold position."

The call to stop came from Brick who was pulling rear security as they traversed the steep rocky slope. They were currently about two-thirds of the way to the top when the urgent message came over the radio.

"What is it?"

"I can see light down on the valley floor."

No sooner had he said it when Cara saw them for herself. Four lights swept the floor of the valley. Beside her Axe raised his night scope to his eye and swept the area below. "There's probably about twenty of them, ma'am." He then said, "Oh shit."

"What is it?"

"There's a technical further back. It must have come up with them. That's crude. It has a mortar mounted on the back of it."

"Not what we need," Cara said. "Let's keep moving."

Below them, the Taliban kept on their track along the floor of the valley while looking for any sign of the invaders. Meanwhile, Cara kept her people climbing the slope. They were just below the crest of the ridgeline when she said to Axe, "This is you. Find a good LUP and sit tight."

"I don't like it, ma'am," he said to Cara.

"What's wrong?"

"We're already having trouble with comms. Putting the top of the ridge between us might create more problems. I'd prefer to be on top if that's OK with you?"

Cara nodded, cursing inwardly for not foreseeing the problem herself. "Do it."

Once the team crested the ridge, Axe dropped out and set himself up with the M110CSASS while the others slipped down the reverse slope to prepare for their ambush.

———————

Jaipur, India

Havildar Feroz Bawa looked at the men around him as the enclosed truck bounced over one of many holes in the asphalt street. Gone were their uniforms, replaced now by black clothing with no identifying insignia. Each man was armed with an AK-47, the universal weapon of choice for terrorists, as well as extra ammunition. Also, certain members of the team had explosives which would be used to cover entries and exits. These would be blown upon their exfiltration. Behind them in the second truck, were more men who were armed the same as those in the first.

The trucks swung into the driveway of the Crown Ramada Hotel and roared along it. The hotel was set on three acres of land, set back off the road a piece to ensure the privacy of their guests.

Bawa looked down at his watch. It was five in the morning. Another thirty minutes and the sun would be up. As it was, there were pink fingers of light on the eastern horizon.

The two trucks came to a stop outside the main entrance to the hotel. The night porter hurried outside, responding to the noisy arrival of the vehicles, a stern expression on his face. He stared dumbly at the first driver who had just climbed from the cab, disbelief on his face that the man didn't know where he was supposed to go. "You cannot park there, you imbecile. All of the deliveries go around to the side."

Ignoring him, the driver walked around the back of the truck and undid the doors. Bawa and his men disembarked from the cargo area, and the man's protests died mid-sentence. The AK in Bawa's hands came up, and he squeezed the trigger, its rattle splitting the early morning serenity. The bullets from the machine gun stitched a pattern across the night porter's chest, and he was dead before he hit the driveway.

Bawa turned to the rest of his men and began barking orders. They ran forward up the few stairs and entered the hotel. Before the Havildar even reached the entrance, more muzzles flashed, and gunfire could be heard.

The bodies of three night-staff lay on the floor of the lobby. Bawa looked at his second in command, a bearded man named Hasan Alvi. He said, "Take ten men and clear the floors. Bring all the guests to the dining hall. If any cause trouble, kill them. When you find Sharma, separate him from the rest. We must get him out of here if it is the last thing we do."

Alvi nodded. "It will be done."

The man hurried away moments later, followed by the ten men he'd chosen. Bawa called another man over. "Put the explosives over the entrance. Then have the other exits done. You have fifteen minutes."

A cry of alarm was followed by the appearance of two of Bawa's men escorting a terrified hotel employee. They stopped in front of the Havildar who stared at the frightened man for a moment before he said, "You will go out and tell the police when they arrive, that we have put explosives at each of the doors and that we will detonate them if anyone tries to enter. Do you understand?"

Relief flooded the man's face as he realized they weren't going to kill him. He nodded furiously, and Bawa said, "Take him away."

"Bawa," another of the Havildar's men called out to him.

He turned to see a heavily mustached man approaching him with a sheet of paper.

"What is it?"

"There are six Americans, five English, seven Dutch, plus various other westerners."

Bawa took the paper and studied it. "Look at these two. They are Indian Generals. Have them separated from the others. We will make a statement while we are here."

More gunfire sounded. Bawa reached down for his hand-held radio. He pressed the talk button and said, "Alvi, what is happening?"

Nothing happened. "Alvi? Alvi? Talk to me."

But there was no reply.

Crown Ramada Hotel
Jaipur, India

Kane stared down at the body before him who he now figured to be Alvi, whoever Alvi was. The head lolled to one side at an odd angle where Kane had broken the neck. He bent down and picked up the

AK and then grabbed some extra magazines.

He'd been asleep when the shooting had started, but there was nothing like the sound of gunfire to bring you out of a deep slumber. At first, he'd just sat up and listened. After climbing from his bed, he'd crossed to the window and peered out through the curtain to see the two trucks. It was only a matter of putting two and two together; it added up to a terrorist attack.

Kane quickly got dressed and then moved to the door. He opened it a crack, and when he saw the hallway was clear, he hurried along to Thurston's room. He was about to knock when the heavy wood door opened and the general stood before him, dressed in jeans and T-shirt.

"It woke you too, huh?" she said.

"Bet my balls it's a terrorist attack," Kane told her.

The next door along the hallway opened, and Traynor appeared. He too was dressed. In his hand was a letter opener.

"Going to take down a few with that?" Kane asked him.

"It was all I could find since the general here wouldn't let me bring a damned handgun," the ex-DEA agent growled.

"Don't cut yourself with it," Thurston joked.

"I'll try not to."

"How do you want to play this, ma'am?" Kane asked her.

"No doubt they'll be going through the floors one at a time. We need to split up and try to save as many as we can."

"Where do we take them, though?"

"The roof?" Traynor proposed.

"I have a better idea," Kane told her. "Let Pete and I loose. We'll see if we can thin them out some."

"With no weapon and a letter opener?"

"We'll manage. Do you have your cell?"

"Yes."

"Pete?"

"Sure."

"All right. Put them on conference call, and we'll use them for comms with our earpieces."

They quickly set them up, and once it was done, Thurston said, "You two be careful."

"Always, ma'am," Kane assured her. "We'll buy you as much time as we can so you can get the people up onto the roof."

She shook her head. "I'm taking them out the back way. There's a fire escape at the rear."

Traynor held out the letter opener in a weak gesture. "You want this?"

Thurston shook her head. "No, you keep it. I might cut myself."

He pulled a face. "Ha, ha, very funny."

"I thought so."

"All right let's do it," Kane said.

At which point they went their separate ways and

was how Kane killed his first terrorist.

"You there, Reaper?" Traynor asked.

"Yeah."

"I got rid of one guy," he informed Kane. "I got me an AK. There was something else, though."

"What's that?"

"This terrorist had explosives on him."

Kane was already moving along the hallway on the seventh floor. "Where are you?"

"On the eighth floor in the stairwell."

"Wait there, I'm on my way."

Kane broke out into the stairwell and climbed the stairs until he reached the eighth-floor landing where he found Traynor and the dead terrorist with the letter opener stuck in his throat. "I guess that came in handy after all."

Kane knelt beside the dead man and checked the explosives. Then he stood up and said, "He was definitely going to do something with the stuff."

"But what? The only thing above us is the roof."

It suddenly dawned on Kane that the rooftop was the man's destination. The doorway onto it, anyway. "Son of a bitch. He was going to rig the door onto the rooftop to explode so if anyone tried to get in that way it would blow. We have to warn the general."

"Good luck with that, she's been out of contact ever since we split up."

"Fuck it," Kane snarled.

Suddenly a door slammed somewhere below

them. Then came the sound of footsteps on the concrete stairs. Kane motioned for Traynor to move through the doorway and into the hallway of the eighth floor. The ex-DEA man pushed the door open and moved through the opening. Kane followed, and the two hurried about a third of the way along the carpeted floor to where there were two recesses on either side in the wall design big enough to conceal a man. They slipped in and waited for the terrorists to come to them.

A few minutes later, the door to the stairwell opened. Several heartbeats later the sound of the latch closing echoed along the hallway. Kane counted off numbers in his head before stepping out into the open, the AK up to his shoulder.

The two men in the hallway froze as the American suddenly appeared before them, taking them completely by surprise. Kane squeezed the trigger of the AK, which rattled off a burst of fire that punched into the first terrorist's chest.

Without waiting to see the result, the Team Reaper commander shifted his aim and fired again. The second terrorist was a little faster at recovering than his friend, and when the 7.62mm rounds from Kane's weapon hammered into him, he was already depressing the trigger on his own weapon.

The long burst of gunfire tracked up the side wall, smashing what looked to be a very expensive picture and frame. It then kept rising until it did the same diagonally across the ceiling, raining down plaster dust before the shooter fell onto his back and the trigger-finger released.

"That'll wake them up well and truly," Traynor said.

Kane nodded. "General, can you hear me?"

A dark silence came back through the cell.

"She won't hear you. It's like she's in some kind of black spot."

"She needs to know about the explosives."

"Agreed, but –"

A beeping sound interrupted what Traynor was about to say. They both looked at their cell screens. The terrorists had jammed the signals.

Thurston and the ten people she'd collected along the way had reached the kitchen without any trouble. Most of the guests had been rounded up as the terror-ists swept the floors. However, a few managed to slip through the nets, and they were the ones with her.

"Keep moving," she said to the frightened people with her. "The doorway will be through the door at the other end."

Her aim had been to use the fire escape, but the attackers had reached it before they did, so she'd changed tack for the kitchen. Now they were almost home free.

"What makes you think that this exit will be any different to the other one," a tall American asked her. "Do you actually know what you are doing?"

The man's name was George, or at least that's what his wife had called him. But he was just a pain in the ass, and if he'd been on his own, Thurston might even have left the bastard behind.

"George," his wife said in a soft voice. "She seems to know what she is doing. Leave it be."

"I ain't too sure, Margaret. We're putting a lot of faith in this damned woman."

"This damned woman has got you this far," Thurston snapped. "So how about you shut up and –"

Thurston never got any further because a man armed with an AK-47 appeared in the doorway of the kitchen behind them. "Hey! What are you doing?" he cried out in heavily accented English. Cries of alarm emanated from a few of the guests.

Thurston took a couple of steps toward him as the guests retreated to the rear of the kitchen. She heard George say, "Lot of fucking good she is."

The armed man approached Thurston, weapon raised. "What are you doing here?" he demanded again.

"We got lost," she said, stopping beside a workbench.

"You were trying to escape."

"No, no."

The AK rose threateningly. "You lie!"

"I'm not lying."

The killer's eyes grew wide, and his anger took over. "Yes! You lie! You lie!"

As he screeched his words, he stepped closer to the general. He was so intent on berating her, he never realized his mistake.

Thurston's left hand shot out and knocked the gun barrel aside. Her right hand looped over, balled into a fist. It crashed against the surprised man's jaw and stunned him. The AK fell from the man's grasp and rattled on the tile floor.

Drawing on her time as a Ranger, the general stepped in close and struck the killer in the throat. He gagged and took a couple of steps back. Thurston followed him and hit him again in the face. However, it was only a glancing blow, and the killer lashed out with his right hand and caught her a lucky blow across the face.

The general's eyes watered, blurring her vision. She staggered back, blinking her eyes furiously, trying to clear them. The man rushed forward and hit her hard as he wrapped his arms around her middle.

Pain shot through Thurston's back as the pair crashed into a stainless-steel bench. The cell and earpiece fell to the floor and smashed. The general raised her fists and then brought them crashing down on her attacker's back. He grunted but never let go. Thurston repeated her actions which forced the man to loosen his grip. She was about to hit him again when he brought his head up, and the back of it connected with her chin.

Thurston reeled around and fell across the bench. She winced with the pain and tasted blood in her mouth. Her eyes scanned the benchtop and then locked onto the handle of the kitchen knife. She reached out for it and suddenly felt herself being dragged away from the weapon.

The man violently spun Thurston around, and clawed hands reached for her throat. The general felt them begin to squeeze and knew that should she fail to remove them, then it would be all over.

In desperation, Thurston brought up her right knee. She felt her attacker stiffen and let out a stifled grunt. His hands loosened, and Thurston broke free, twisted around.

Her right hand fixed on the handle of the knife and brought it sweeping around. The sharp blade drove deep into the attacker's throat slicing through the flesh with ease. The man reeled back; the knife still embedded. His eyes were wide with shock, and he reached up, his own hand grasping at the handle.

Somehow, he managed to pull the weapon free and with it came a torrent of blood spurting out onto the floor. The killer gave Thurston a weird look and then collapsed onto the floor where he bled out quickly.

Gasping for breath, the general turned and stared at George. Through gritted teeth, she growled, "You were saying, asshole?"

George said nothing.

"Now that is taken care of, shall we get the hell

out of here?"

Thurston looked down at the smashed cell on the floor and cursed inwardly. She dismissed it and walked toward the back of the kitchen once more, still trembling from her exertions. Walking through the doorway and out into the small area where the deliveries were made, she approached the exit and took one look before saying, "Fuck it."

Turning back toward the group, she said, "Everybody, turn around."

"What for?" George snarled. "The door is there. I'm getting the fuck out."

"Go right ahead if you want to die. They've wired it to explode."

"So, what do you suggest we do, Sheena of the Jungle?"

"I suggest you shut up before I leave your ass behind."

Thurston shoved past him and walked back to the dead man on the floor. Reaching down, she found a hand-held radio and then picked up the AK-47 along with some extra ammunition. Their only option was to hunker down in a room somewhere and wait.

Unfortunately, the group never made it out of the kitchen before two men appeared in the entrance doorway. Both were armed with guns which were pointed right at the general.

Thurston dropped the AK and cursed out loud once more. "Fuck it, I knew coming to India was a bad idea."

CHAPTER FOUR

Afghanistan-Pakistan Border

"Reaper Two? Bravo Three. Your target is approximately one klick out from your position, over."

"Copy that, Bravo Three," Cara said into her comms. "Axe, you get that?"

"Tell them to hurry up, ma'am. I don't think these guys on the other side of the mountain got the memo."

"Why? What have you got?"

"I have maybe twenty Taliban climbing rapidly toward my position. The vehicle with the mortar mounted on it has stopped at the foot of the slope. If it has the range, they'll be able to drop them on top of the ridge and on the reverse slope where you are."

"Roger, keep an eye on them."

"Yes, ma'am."

"Bravo Three, how many tangos with the pack train?"

"Looks to be six, Reaper Two."

"Copy."

Cara gathered Brick and Arenas around her. "The pack train isn't that far out. There are six tangos with them. We need to pick our targets and take them down quickly. And try not to hit the horses. I damned well like horses."

"Yes, ma'am."

"Bravo One, copy?"

"Copy, Reaper Two."

"I've got a job for you if you're up for it?"

"Roger."

"I want you to hit the Taliban on the far side of the ridge when we hit the pack train. Make your target the technical. The last thing we need is them lobbing rounds over the ridge on top of us."

"We'll take care of it for you."

"Thanks. Out."

Now they waited. Watched and waited. Twenty minutes passed before the pack train came into view along the valley floor. Cara reached out to Axe once more. "How you looking, Axe?"

"Another ten mikes and they'll be on top of me."

"As soon as I give the order, you're weapons-free."

"Yes, ma'am. Just don't take too long."

"Copy that."

"Bravo One, standby."

"Copy, Reaper Two."

The pack train snaked its way along the narrow

valley. One of the Taliban was leading the horses at the head of the column. There were two more on each side, and the other three brought up the rear. All were armed with AK-47s.

Cara said, "Pick your targets. We'll take the lead tango and the two flankers first. All shooters cleared hot on my mark. Bravo One, you go on three."

At the altitude the UAV was flying it would take the Hellfire missile mere seconds before it impacted on the technical.

"Ready…"

"Three…"

Back at the ops center, Reynolds hit the fire button for the Hellfire.

"Two…"

They all picked their targets.

"One…"

Each shooter let out a long breath.

"Execute."

Fingers tightened on triggers, and the first volley of gunfire was released. The lead tango's head jerked back as a round from Cara's 416 slammed home. The two flankers dropped at the same time as well, both wounds mortal.

The three of them shifted aim and fired again. All within a few heartbeats, catching the second lot of targets fully unaware.

Meanwhile, up on the ridge, Axe squeezed off a shot with the M110A1. The 7.62mm round blew out of the barrel and punched into the chest of the lead Taliban insurgent at almost the same time that the Hellfire impacted the technical.

The Taliban fighter threw up his arms against a backdrop of black and orange. The sound of the explosion rolled up the slope in a solid wave. Axe shifted his aim and concentrated on the next closest insurgent and dropped him where he stood.

Gunfire erupted from below as the Taliban opened fire upon the crest of the ridge. The screams of ricochets filled the morning air while a large black smudge rose into the sky. Axe shifted his aim and shot another fighter before ducking down below the ridgeline.

He pressed his talk button on his comms and said, "I could use another gun up here."

"I'll send Brick up," Cara replied.

"Yes, ma'am."

The gunfire from the Taliban grew fiercer, and the big ex-recon marine knew instantly they were about to assault his position. Then the call came through from Teller about the UAV.

"Reaper Two, we have a problem with the UAV."

Cara pressed her talk button as she moved down the slope toward the ambush site. "What is it, Bravo Three?"

"The vehicle is unresponsive. It looks like it's about to crash to the east of your position."

Cara cursed under her breath, then said, "How far east?"

"Maybe five klicks on its downward trajectory."

"That's inside Pakistan, Bravo Three."

"Yes, ma'am."

"Reaper Two, this is Zero."

"Copy, Zero."

"You need to get those drugs dealt with and then exfil east to secure the crash site, over."

Great. Things were getting shitty again. "Don't they have people for that, Zero?"

"Not as close as you, Reaper Two. Special forces will be sending a team to assist you, but their trek is worse than yours, and you'll reach the site before they do," Ferrero told her.

"Are we sure the UAV is a lost cause?"

"From where I sit," Teller said, "there ain't no coming back."

"Copy that. Reaper Two, out."

Cara turned to look at Arenas. "Can you deal with those drugs?"

"Yes, ma'am."

"Save some of those explosives. We're going to need them. I'm going back up the ridge."

"Copy that."

Crown Ramada Hotel
Jaipur, India

Bullets chewed chunks of plaster from the ornately

decorated walls of the hallway, showering the plush carpet with a fine layer of white powder. One of the attackers lay on the floor already coated in the stuff.

"Imagine what this shit does to your lungs," Traynor called out from opposite Kane in the door opening.

The Team Reaper commander leaned out from his cover and squeezed off another burst at the remaining two shooters further along the hallway. "I'm trying not to."

The hand-held radio in Kane's pocket screamed at him once more as the person on the other end demanded answers as to what was happening.

Both men were on the fourth floor. After having dodged a couple of roving patrols, their luck had finally run out. Now they were involved in a ferocious firefight with two seemingly well-trained men.

"These guys aren't ordinary terrorists, Reaper!" Traynor shouted.

"No. They're military. Have to be."

Kane leaned out to fire again but was driven back by a long fusillade. Once it had stopped, he managed to fire some more rounds before the magazine ran dry. He dropped the banana clip on the floor next to the other one and slapped the last one home. "Last mag, Pete."

"Yeah, me too. What's the plan?"

It was then that the decision was taken out of their hands.

———————

Thurston was shoved roughly in front of Bawa who stared at her with curious eyes. But before speaking to her, he asked her captors in his native tongue, "Where is Sharma?"

One of the men shrugged. "We do not know."

"Find him. He is in the hotel somewhere. Where is Alvi?"

Another shrug which seemed to anger Bawa even more than he already was. "Go, get out of my sight!"

Thurston looked around the large hall while Bawa talked with his men. After a quick mental calculation, she figured there could be up to seventy people packed in there. Which all in all, considering the hotel could take five-hundred guests comfortably, wasn't too bad. Or was it. How full had the hotel been? How many were already dead?

"Who are you?"

Thurston looked at him for a drawn-out moment before answering. "Nobody. Who are you?"

"I will ask the questions."

"Suit yourself."

Bawa studied her some more then she saw an idea flicker in his eyes. "You are not like them."

"Like who?"

"The ones who sit and cower because they are afraid."

"If you say so."

"I am thinking that you are American military," Bawa theorized.

"What makes you say that?"

"I can tell."

"They say it takes one to know one."

The Pakistani nodded. "They do."

"Who are you? You aren't Indian. That would make you from Pakistan. Am I right?"

"Are they your people?" Bawa asked, deflecting.

"Are who my people?"

"Those that are killing my men."

"Why are you here?"

With a nod of his head, Bawa looked at one of his men. "Get one of them."

The man disappeared and then returned with one of the Indian generals. Thurston recognized him straight away. It was the one she knew as Manish Joshi. He was one of the ones she had flown here to see. He stared at her without so much as a glimmer of recognition in his eyes. Bawa took out his sidearm and shot the general in the head.

The crash of the weapon bounced around the walls of the enclosed space, the absence of acoustic properties failing to absorb the noise and brought about panicked cries from those within. The Pakistani said, "I have another general in the other room. He will meet the same fate if you do not start to cooperate."

Thurston looked down at the dead Indian, blood

starting to pool around his head. Inside she felt her anger thrashing around, and she tried not to let it show.

Bawa gave her a cold smile. "Good, you are angry. Now, who are those people?"

"The general is a soldier like you and me. He expects to die," Thurston told him.

The Pakistani nodded. "Maybe you are right."

The gun came up again and barked. The 9mm bullet from the weapon cut through the air and punched into the chest of the man Thurston knew as the loudmouth, George. He grunted and fell back; his wife knelt over him, screaming.

"Fucking asshole," Thurston hissed and made to go to the fallen man. Suddenly one of Bawa's men stood in front of her and blocked her passage. The general brought up her knee into his unprotected groin, and a moment later, he was writhing in pain on the floor.

Thurston stepped over him, half expecting a bullet between her shoulder blades, but it never came. She knelt beside George and ripped open his shirt.

"Help him, please," his wife pleaded.

The man was bleeding out before Thurston's eyes, and she knew she had to prevent that from happening or he would die. She reached out and grabbed George's wife's hand and said, "Do this. Stick your finger in the hole."

"What?"

Thurston sighed and took the woman's finger and stuck it in the wound. Her husband cried out in pain, but the general made sure he couldn't rise. "Keep it there until I get back."

She stood up and glanced around. "You, give me your shirt."

A slim man wearing a light-blue shirt hesitated.

"Now," Thurston demanded.

He went to take it off when the room filled with the sound of gunfire again. The man's head whip-lashed back as he fell backward violently.

Thurston whirled, eyes blazing. *"You fucking ass-hole!"* she screeched.

"Answer my question, or I will kill another one. Are they here with you?"

"Yes! Damn it, they are."

———————

"Reaper, can you hear me?"

Kane looked down at the hand-held radio as another hail of bullets ripped along the hallway. He drew back and retrieved it from where it was tucked away, raising it to his mouth.

"Copy, ma'am."

"We have a small problem, Reaper."

"How's that, General?"

There was a long pause, and another voice came over the radio. This time it was a man's and Kane recognized it as the one he'd kept hearing before. "Mister Reaper or whatever your name is. We have your friend and will kill her if you do not surrender to us immediately."

"Where are you?" Kane asked, trying to buy a little time.

"In the main hall."

"OK. We'll be there soon."

Anger started to boil inside Kane and, opting not to suppress it, it suddenly came to the surface, and the 'Reaper' came out to play.

Kane stepped out from cover shrouded in white. The AK in his hands opened up with brutal efficiency as he stood there, seemingly bulletproof. Two Pakistani Special Forces renegades were surprised by his move. Both died with a look of bewilderment as the heavy caliber slugs snatched away their lives.

"What the hell was that, Reaper?" Traynor asked him, baffled by his team leader's actions.

Kane stared at him, face grim. "They've got Thurston."

Afghanistan-Pakistan Border

Bullets flashed overhead as Cara dropped down beside Axe and Brick. Down the slope, she could see the Taliban moving left and right as they zigzagged up the steep rise. "How are we looking?"

"They're pretty willing, ma'am," Axe told her as the M110A1 slammed back into his shoulder once more.

"You heard the last transmission?"

"Yes, ma'am. Only problem is if we disengage, we're going to have them crawling up our asses in no time, and they'll have the high ground."

Cara ran her gaze over the ground once more then pressed her talk button. "Zero? Reaper Two. Are there any air assets up and in our region at the moment?"

"Wait one, Reaper Two."

More gunfire rippled along the slope below them. Brick kept up a steady rhythm with his 416 just with it on semi-auto. Suddenly the slope below them erupted in a burst of orange filled with large chunks of rock and debris. The soundwave rippled up the ridge and washed over the three Team Reaper operators.

"Fuck! Mortar," Axe growled just as another round landed. "The bastards moved another one in."

"Where is it?" Cara snapped.

Another round came in, this one closer as it was walked up the slope toward them. "The bastards are zeroing in on us," Brick called out.

"Find their spotter."

"I got the mortar," Axe said. "They've set it up just below the reverse side of the ridge opposite."

"Shit," Cara growled. "Zero, do we have any news on air assets yet?"

"A pair of A-10s have just been scrambled, Reaper Two. ETA your position in ten mikes."

Behind her on the valley floor, Cara heard Arenas detonate the explosives. She turned to look and saw the leftovers of the explosion. Then she turned her attention back to her current predicament just in time for another mortar round to land virtually on top of them.

Cara felt herself being tossed through the air by the concussive wave of the mortar blast. Time seemed to be suspended as everything slowed down. As reality came crashing back, pain slammed through her body as she landed, air whooshing from her lungs. Blackness threatened to take her from the present, but she fought the urge to let it overwhelm her.

The coppery taste of blood flooded Cara's mouth, and she felt a pair of hands grab her roughly. "Don't fight me, ma'am."

Through the ringing in her ears, she recognized Brick's voice then felt herself being dragged. Once they had stopped, she looked up into his face. The Team Reaper medic smiled at her and said, "At least you're still awake. How are you feeling?"

"Like shit."

"Just lay there while I check you out. Open your mouth."

"What?"

"Open your mouth. I want to see where the blood is coming from."

Cara felt his fingers open her mouth as he looked around inside. "It's just your tongue. You must have bitten it when you landed."

Another mortar round landed. CRUMP!

Brick heard it coming and placed his body over Cara's. Rocks and debris rained down on top of them after which, Brick rose again and started to examine her once more.

After a minute or so, the medic gave a grunt and said, "I think you're OK. Just wait there for a few minutes before you get up."

CRUMP!

"Brick, find that fucking spotter."

"Yes, ma'am."

Axe's voice came over the comms. "If you two are finished playing doctors and nurses, I think that it may be wise to haul ass out of here. Another truck-load of Taliban just pulled up."

Brick stuck out his hand. "I guess we'll find out whether or not you're OK together."

"I guess we will."

Cara winced as she came to her feet, but after a moment of adjustment, she seemed to be none the worse for wear.

CRUMP!

Cara and Brick ducked as earth showered them once again. They started back to the crest of the ridge where Axe was sited. She peered over the rise and into the valley below just in time to see yet another truck arrive and park next to the other.

"OK," Cara said with a nod. "Let's get the hell out of here."

CHAPTER FIVE

Afghanistan-Pakistan Border

The two A-10s burned low overhead with a deafening noise. They were so close Cara thought that if she were atop the ridges which surrounded them, she could just about touch the machines.

"About time," she growled as another hailstorm of bullets kicked up dirt around her position. The Taliban now had the high ground of the ridge and had forced them into cover behind some large rocks.

Cara's comms crackled to life, and a voice filled her head, "Reaper Two, this is Cobra lead, come in, over."

"Copy, Cobra, good to see you."

"Ma'am, we're a flight of two here for your assistance. Just tell us where to start, and we'll go to work."

"Copy, Cobra Lead. We'll pop some smoke and

guide you in from there."

"Copy. Awaiting smoke."

Cara turned to Arenas who reached down and took an M18 colored smoke grenade from his webbing. He then pulled the pin and tossed it out into the clear. After a few seconds, a thick red cloud started to billow up from it. Cobra Lead, smoke popped. Say again, smoke is popped."

"Copy that, Reaper Two. I see red smoke, confirm."

"Affirmative, Cobra Lead."

"Copy. Where do you want it, Reaper Two?"

"There's a ridge above us running east-west. They're dug in up there giving us what for."

"Copy, keep your heads down. Cobra Lead inbound cleared hot."

The two A-10s came in hard and fast. Powered by two General Electric TF34-GE-100A turbofans, the Thunderbolt had a maximum speed of three hundred and eighty-one knots. Their armory was awesome.

The screaming turbofans shook the valley walls and then a long BRRRRRP! seemed to rip the overhead air apart like a giant rending a thick velvet curtain. The 30 mm GAU-8/A Avenger rotary cannon made the top of the ridgeline explode with violent geysers of earth erupting skyward as they drove deep down. Then it was over, the first A-10 had come and gone.

"Cobra Two inbound and cleared hot."

Cara expected more of the same, however, this time was different. An AGM-65 Maverick air-to-surface missile lanced across the sky. "Your friends will have to walk home, Reaper Two. We're coming around for another run. Cobra Lead out."

The valley went eerily quiet for a handful of heartbeats before the high-pitched scream of the turbofans could be heard once more. Again, the rotary cannon opened up issuing violent death. Without a visual of what was happening upon the ridge, the sound was all they had to go on, which was something akin to a severe hailstorm. Only this one would kill you.

The second plane came in and plastered the ridgeline with more hellfire and brimstone. Then it pulled up and joined its flight leader.

"Reaper Two? Cobra Lead. Our job here is done. Have a nice day."

"Copy, Cobra Lead. Thanks for your help."

The sound of the A-10s receded into the distance, and Cara tentatively stood erect. She moved out into the open and braced herself. When nothing happened, she said, "All right, let's move. Brick, you're on point."

"Yes, ma'am."

"Zero, copy?"

"Copy, Reaper Two."

"We're moving out toward the border. We'd appreciate any help you can give us."

"I'll get Slick and Teller onto it and see what they can come up with."

"Roger. Reaper Two out."

Crown Ramada Hotel
Jaipur, India

Kane moved swiftly through the suite and out onto the balcony. Already there were lights flashing everywhere from the Indian police. Trucks had gathered as well, which he presumed meant that the ATS, Anti-terrorism Squad was onsite too; a force inspired by Los Angeles SWAT.

"What are you doing, Reaper?" Traynor asked.

Kane said nothing, just shifted his gaze down over the rail. He studied the side of the hotel for a moment and looked back up.

"Kane?"

"We're going down."

"Over the balcony?"

"Yes."

"I've heard about you and spontaneous shit like this."

Kane looked at him and smiled. "Keeps the relationship interesting."

"I like it just the way it is."

Slinging the AK over his shoulder, Kane started

to climb over the railing. "Come on, the last one down is a … whoa!"

Kane suddenly disappeared. A horrified expression crossed Traynor's face as he lunged for the rail. He peered down over the side and saw his friend hanging by one hand from the next balcony rail down. Kane gave him a wry smile. "Watch that first step."

"Crazy son of a bitch."

Traynor climbed over and followed him down to the second floor. Once they both reached the balcony, Kane tried the sliding glass door. It was locked. He unslung the AK and was just positioning it when Traynor said, "Just hold up there, Slash, before you go killing a harmless door."

The ex-DEA agent stepped forward and placed his hands on either side of the glass. "Before I became a UC for Uncle Sam, I had to make ends meet. Had me a job installing these things."

He gave a grunt, and the door slid open. Kane stared at him and said, "How'd you do that?"

"Magic."

They stepped inside and hurried through the suite to the door. Traynor mentioned to Kane as they went, "You never said what we were going to do."

"I don't really know."

"All I know is that he's got Thurston in the main hall. That's where he wants us to go."

The hand-held radio crackled to life. "Are you

there, Mister Reaper?"

Kane cursed as he retrieved it and pressed the talk button. "Yes, I'm here."

"What is taking you so long to get here?"

"I took a shortcut that wasn't actually a shortcut."

"You are wasting my time, Mister Reaper," the voice said resignedly. "I don't like my time being wasted."

The report of a shot filtered through the radio along with cries of fear and alarm. Then the man came back on and said laconically, "You have five minutes, or another dies."

———————

"We have found him, Feroz," a thin man said to Bawa's back.

The Pakistani turned and looked at the man standing between his escort. Sharma cringed under the hard stare. "It is good to see you, Professor."

"Who – who are you?" Sharma stammered.

"You will see."

"Feroz, you should go. Let us finish what we started."

Bawa averted his gaze and looked at the man who'd spoken. "You are not coming, Farid?"

The man shook his head. "Our journey will end here so that you will survive to finish the mission. We have come prepared."

The Pakistani stared at the other man and nodded. "You feel this way too?"

"Yes."

"Too bad. You will come with me," Bawa ordered before turning back to Farid. "You will be remembered as a man of honor, Farid. I am pleased to have you serve in my command. I will be sure to let Colonel Khan know that you died gloriously."

Bawa snapped a sharp salute which was returned by the man in front of him. "If the Americans appear," the Havildar said, "kill them."

"With pleasure."

"Javed, bring him."

A short distance away, Thurston took time to process what she was seeing and hearing. She studied the prisoner, his fear, and then the reaction of Bawa. Next, she watched as the three of them left the room. The man who'd brought the prisoner in with the other snapped a couple of orders and then called out to another terrorist across the room.

He leaned down and picked up two duffel bags, carrying them across to where Farid stood. He placed them on the floor, and she watched as he unzipped them both.

When he reached inside, exposing the contents, Thurston's blood ran cold with what she saw. They had explosive vests. Four of them, which they passed out amongst those who were in the hall.

———————

"Hey!" Traynor yelled, and the terrorist whirled about, bringing up his weapon. But before the man could fire, Kane stepped up behind him and bashed him up the side of his head with the butt of the AK. The man slumped to the floor, out cold.

They dragged the body into the room beside them and closed the door.

"That's another taken care of, but we're running out of time here," the ex-DEA man said.

Kane nodded. "You're right. Get his clothes on."

"What?"

"He's your size, get them on. I have a plan."

"If you're going to do what I think you are, then you're crazy. We haven't even got the same color skin."

"I didn't say it was perfect," Kane told him and took up the radio again. "We'll be there in a moment."

A few heartbeats and a voice said, "I'll be waiting."

It wasn't the same. The voice sounded different.

A few minutes later, Traynor was changed and said, "Now what?"

Kane bent down and grabbed the handgun which had been carried by his last victim. It was a Berretta. He checked it and then tucked it in his pants at the small of his back. Then he placed his thumbs in either side of it as though he had his hands tied and said, "Let's go."

Thurston watched as the men put on their explosive vests and tucked the firing triggers into their pockets where they could be easily accessed. Her mind whirled as she tried to figure out a plan with an outcome where she or anyone else in the room didn't wind up dead, blown into little pieces by the killers.

It seemed useless, and for someone like her, each was an unacceptable scenario. But there must be a way.

She studied them some more, looking for any weakness in their defenses. Then Thurston shook her head. Who was she kidding? It would take something superhuman to get it done.

And right then, superhuman delivered.

"Shit!" Kane hissed in a low tone. "The bastards have suicide vests on."

"Just means we'll have to shoot straighter and quicker," Traynor whispered. "No turning back now. How many you see?"

"Four."

"I see you found our friend," Farid called across the room not able to see the man behind Kane because the Team Reaper leader was blocking his view.

"Get me a bit closer," Kane murmured.

"Where is the other one? There were two," Farid pressed.

"You ready?" Kane asked.

"Just shoot straight," Traynor replied.

The terrorist frowned. "Well? Answer me."

"Let's do this," the ex-DEA agent said and then stepped to the side.

Kane's right hand was already wrapped around the butt of the handgun tucked into the waistband of his pants. It swept around and up like the many times he'd practiced on the firing range over his military years.

The weapon barked, and Farid's head snapped back, a hole in his forehead. Relying on instinct, Kane switched target and fired again as the second bomber fumbled to get his hand into his pocket where the trigger was.

Another bullseye.

Beside Kane, Traynor fired the AK, and the top of a third terrorist's head came apart with the 7.62mm slug. That left one man with a vest.

One man whose hand dived into his pocket and came out with a handful of a trigger. He closed his eyes and squeezed.

Kane froze for the first time in his life under fire as he waited for his world to be torn apart by nails, bolts, nuts, or whatever the hell they had inside the vests.

Nothing happened.

The Team Reaper leader saw the hand press again, and again, and again. But before it happened once more, Kane shot him.

"Pete, your left!" Thurston shouted.

Traynor swung the AK around, and as soon as the foresight settled on the chest of another terrorist, he squeezed the trigger. Twice.

The man threw up his arms and collapsed to the floor as the gunfire rocked the hall once more. Both men swept the room, searching for more targets. When they failed to locate any, they converged on Thurston. "Are there any more, General?" Kane asked.

She nodded. "I think there are somewhere. But we need to get these people out of here. Can one of you defuse a bomb?"

"Sure," Kane said in a condescending tone. "I did one yesterday."

"Then it looks like we take them out a window."

A howl of despair reached Thurston's ears, and she turned to look in the direction from which it had emanated. George's wife was crouched over his motionless form. The general muttered something under her breath and then said to her two operators, "Get us the hell out of here, Reaper."

Afghanistan-Pakistan Border

The four Team Reaper personnel lay belly down atop the rocky ridge looking down at the scene below them. A truckload of ten armed men had set up a perimeter around the crash site where the UAV had come down, while two others examined the wreckage for anything usable.

"Zero, looks like we're a little late to the party, over," Cara said into her comms.

"Copy, Reaper Two. We have a satellite tasked over your area, and the pictures are coming through now."

"Copy that. Awaiting orders."

The team was now two kilometers inside Pakistan which was bad news for them if they were caught by the home team's military. Because even though the two countries were on reasonable terms, things still hadn't recovered fully since the incursion to get Osama bin Laden.

"They're not Taliban, ma'am," Axe said from beside her as he watched the group through his scope.

"Who then, al-Qa'ida?"

"That would be my guess."

"Zero, my righthand man here is telling me that these guys are al-Qa'ida. Confirm?"

"Wait one, Reaper Two."

"What are they doing, Axe?" Cara asked.

"Just going through the wreckage looking for

stuff to use, ma'am."

"Reaper Two? Zero. We're thinking along the lines that your man is right. These look to be al-Qa'ida. You are cleared to engage."

"Copy, Zero. Any word on our special forces friends?"

"Not as yet."

"Copy. Reaper Two, out."

Cara eased herself back down the ridge to just below the crest and summoned the others to join her. "OK, we're going hot again. Axe just take every target of opportunity you can get a shot at. Priority on the ones sifting through the wreckage. Don't let them get away with anything. The rest of us will just pick them off one at a time until they're all dead or they've run off. Any questions?"

"I have one," Axe said.

"What is it?"

"Do you get rubbed raw around the crotch out here in all this heat? Mine feels like it's on fucking fire about now."

The three of them chuckled, and Cara said, "If you are having too much trouble, I can get Brick to rub some lotion on the area for you."

"No, ma'am, I think I'll be fine."

"Anything else?"

They were quiet.

"OK, Axe, give us a moment to get in position. If we're discovered, then cut loose."

"Yes, ma'am."

Cara, Brick, and Arenas slipped over the crest of the ridge using all the cover they could find to remain concealed. Once they were within range, Cara called a halt. Above them, the sun beat down mercilessly; however, due to them being so high up, there wasn't the heat which there would have been at the lower altitudes.

Cara was about to press her talk button when the area surrounding the crash site below erupted in gunfire. She watched on as the al-Qa'ida fighters below started to cry out and fall.

"What the hell?"

It was over in a heartbeat. All the fighters were down and out of the fight. That was when the shooters emerged from their hiding positions.

"Motherfucker," Axe hissed. "They're Pakistani Special Forces."

"Zero, are you getting this?" Cara asked Ferrero.

"We're seeing it, Reaper Two."

"All Reaper elements hold fire until we work out what the hell is going on," Cara ordered.

"Copy."

"Copy."

"Reaper Five, copy?"

As the team watched on from their positions, they saw the new arrivals check on the dead and sift through the wreckage of the downed UAV. A headcount came up with ten men, all highly trained, without a doubt.

"Reaper Two? Zero."

Cara pressed her talk once more. "Copy, Zero."

"You are to secure the wreckage."

"Ma'am, you need to see this," Axe interrupted.

Cara ignored him to concentrate on what she'd just heard from Ferrero. "Say again, Zero?"

"Your orders are to secure the crash site."

"But these guys are Pakistani," Cara pointed out.

"Ma'am," Axe tried again. "Not all of them."

"What do you mean?"

"I got my eyes on at least one Chinese officer down there," Axe informed her.

"Christ, can this day get any better?"

"That's what I was about to tell you, Reaper Two. We picked up traffic which was inconsistent with what you were reporting. The short of it is that it was coded Chinese, and it originated from your area. That is why you've been ordered to secure the area. If any components fall into their hands … well, you know what's likely to happen."

"What about if we just kill the Chinese officer?" Cara asked.

"It might work. But if it doesn't, you've given your hand away."

"Axe, is there only the one Chinese man down there?"

After a few moments, his voice came back over the comms, "As far as I can tell, ma'am."

"Alright, take him out. Everyone else remain in position and do not fire."

Even though the M110A1 was suppressed, the sound was still audible to those close enough to hear. Down below, the Chinese officer lurched and fell to the ground.

All around the perimeter, voices rang out as the soldiers looked about for the origin of the shot. Cara held her breath as she waited for them to open fire and wildly spray the slope where the team was hidden. The gunfire, however, didn't eventuate. Instead, what happened next was beyond her control.

Once more the valley below them was rocked with the sound of automatic fire, and the Pakistani Special Forces team fell victim to the vicious hail of incoming rounds.

"Reaper Two, what's happening?" Ferrero snapped.

"I don't know, Zero. It isn't us."

The firing stopped suddenly, and the last echoes died away. Cara watched on as a five-man team emerged from their firing positions.

"They're SEALs, ma'am," he informed her. "I'd know squids like that anywhere."

"Zero, it looks like our backup has arrived. Except I think they just took over the mission."

"Copy, Reaper Two."

Cara watched the special operators for a moment longer as they started to check on the fallen Pakistan soldiers. Cara spoke into her comms when she'd seen enough, "Saddle up. We're heading back. Brick, you're on point. Zero, can you organize us a ride for when we're back across the line?"

"Will do, Reaper Two."

"OK. Let's go."

CHAPTER SIX

National Security Agency, Fort Meade, Maryland

Scott Bald opened the door to his boss' office and said, "I think I know where the weapons are."

Miller looked up from his paperwork, leaned back in his chair, and put his pen down before saying, "Do tell. Don't keep me waiting all day."

"They're in Kashmir."

"They what?"

"We've been working the problem, and we believe that they were taken by a man named Adjeet Khan. He's a colonel in the Pakistan SSG. He and some of his more trusted men disappeared some days ago and haven't been seen since. The timing would seem to coincide with the disappearance of the nukes."

"Why would he do something like that?" Miller asked. "Does he have any ties to terror organizations, that we know about?"

"Nothing has flagged yet, sir, but I have people looking into it."

The expression on Miller's face changed suddenly, and he sat up straight in his chair. "You did say Pakistani SSG, right?"

"Yes, sir."

"Do you think there is the possibility of a link to what's happening in India?"

Bald said, "I'll have someone look into it. But about Khan. What are we going to do?"

"Do you have an area of operations nailed down?"

"Yes, sir."

"You realize that sending a covert team into Kashmir could be bad all 'round?"

"Could be worse if we don't find those weapons."

"Send Cunningham and his team. But make sure they understand it is a recon mission only. We need to have a zero footprint if we can."

Bald nodded. "Yes, sir. And if they are discovered?"

"They're on their own. We can't help them."

Incirlik Air Base, Turkey

Rick Cunningham was sick of the damned heat. The solidly built, six-foot-four operator from Kentucky was looking forward to the following day when he and his team would be rotated back to the States for some downtime. They'd been up this time around for four months, and they were tired. After missions into Somalia, Syria, and Iran, it was time for a break. However, one last call from the NSA Field Office was about to change that.

The alarm for an incoming call sounded from the laptop sitting on the table in the team's quarters. All four men stopped what they were doing to turn damning gazes upon it.

"Don't answer the fucking thing," Hank Pullen growled as the lanky Texan came to his feet.

"I'm with Hank," the team's second in command, Jeff Craig agreed.

Bo Randall, a stocky native of the great state of Georgia, pointed his M9 Beretta at the device and snapped, "Let me shoot the fucking thing, Boss."

For a fleeting moment Cunningham was tempted to let him do it, because every time they received encrypted calls over the computer link, it led them into tight situations.

Cunningham sighed and hit one of the keys. The screen came to life with a face that most knew well.

"Hello, Bald," Cunningham greeted the NSA man unenthusiastically. "What kind of shit show do you have for us the day before we rotate out of here?"

"I'm sorry, Rick," Bald said, sounding apologetic.

"For fuck sake, I knew it," Pullen murmured in the background.

Bald continued, "If it could be put off for the new team it would have been."

Cunningham nodded. "I understand. Fill us in."

"We've got an 'Empty Quiver' situation."

Every single man on Cunningham's team moved closer to the laptop, their faces set as hard as granite. Those two words had each man on edge, for 'Empty Quiver' was code for a stolen nuclear weapon.

"I'm thinking that because you've come to us that it is a delicate situation. Is that right?" Cunningham asked.

"You'd be right in thinking that."

"Where are we being sent to?"

"Kashmir."

"Shit," the team leader heard Craig curse.

"Who has the package?"

"Packages. There are two."

"You're kidding. Where did they come from?"

"Pakistan," Bald replied. "They were taken by a Pakistani SSG officer named Ajeet Khan."

"What are we supposed to do with these nukes when we find them?"

"Nothing. It's only a recon mission. Zero footprint if possible, and if not, you're on your own, we can't help you. You understand why?"

Cunningham did. Kashmir was the hottest place on earth. Worse than Syria and Afghanistan for the simple reason that any blowup in the region had a high probability of leading to nuclear war. It also was home to many terrorist organizations because no one wanted to be the one to kick it off.

"When do we leave?" he asked Bald.

"You have two hours to prep. Insertion will be tonight. I'll send through all the information we have. You can look it over on the plane. Sorry, Rick, I know it's not ideal, but it's all we have."

"Understood, sir."

The connection was terminated, and Cunningham ran his gaze over the stoic faces of his men. He said, "Prep your kit and make sure everything is in order before we get on that plane."

There were nods all around. They understood the meaning of his words and the nuance that this time out it was more than a slight possibility that some or all wouldn't come back. Then Bo Randall asked the obvious question, "How the fuck are we meant to get out?"

"I guess that depends," Craig said. "It could well be a long walk home."

"Shit, this isn't going to be good, is it?"

Cunningham nodded. "No, it isn't."

Crown Ramada Hotel
Jaipur, India

"There is no sign of them," Kali Singh, the man in

charge of the ATS told Thurston. "My men have swept the grounds but have come up with nothing. All that we have are the two prisoners from inside the hotel."

"They must have slipped through the net, somehow," the general said.

"So, it would seem. But right now, I have other more important matters to attend to. Like reporting to my superiors that the men who attacked the hotel were Pakistani Special Forces."

Singh spun on his heel and stalked off, calling to one of his subordinates as he went. Kane looked at Thurston and asked, "You look troubled, ma'am. What is it?"

"This wasn't an ordinary terrorist attack," she explained. "Bawa wanted that man he took with him for a reason. He called him Professor. We need to find out who he is and why they took him. The Indian authorities aren't going to look beyond the fact that the bad guys were from Pakistan."

"Sounds like a job for Slick," Traynor said.

"My thoughts exactly."

"I take it that the holiday is over," Kane theorized.

"Correct."

Jaipur Inn, Jaipur

Three hours and one hotel later, Kane emerged from a long, steaming shower and padded out across the plush carpet of his bedroom with just a towel around his waist. When he looked up, he was surprised to see Thurston standing there waiting for him, dressed in her favored jeans and a blue T-shirt. Her hair was loose and still damp from her own shower, and hanging down past her shoulders. She smiled at him and said, "If I'd have known you were having a party, I would have come undressed."

He nodded. "I'm sure you would have been the most popular girl in the room, ma'am."

She stepped in close to him and touched the scar on his chest. "Philippines?"

"Yes, ma'am. Can I help you with something?" he added, changing the focus of where the conversation seemed to be heading.

Thurston turned and walked away before taking a seat on the end of his bed. "I just heard back from Slick. He's managed to track down the identity of our mystery man. His name is Professor Javed Sharma."

Kane nodded. "Why do I get the feeling that the word professor doesn't indicate anything good?"

"Because it isn't. The esteemed professor works in the field of nuclear science."

"Next you'll tell me that he –"

"No, I won't because you already know the answer."

"What about this Bawa? The one who took him?"

"Ex-Pakistani SSG. Slick tried to find out more but ran into roadblocks everywhere that he went. Something is up, and it would appear that no one wants it out in the public domain."

"What about General Jones?"

"Last resort because really this has nothing to do with our purview."

"So, we're just going to let it go?"

"I never said that. I've still got Slick digging around."

"So, where do we go from here?" Kane asked her.

"Back to Afghanistan. It seems there's been substantially increased activity from the Taliban warlords and we're to try and stem the flow of their product across the border."

"What about the DEA FAST teams?"

Thurston shrugged. "I guess we're just good at what we do. Now, put your damned clothes on, and I'll buy you and Pete a beer."

Kane nodded. "Best offer I've had all day."

Thurston raised an eyebrow. "Really?"

Azad Kashmir

During daylight hours, Kashmir was a magnificent picturesque landscape with deep valleys, steep snow-capped peaks that seemed to reach all the way into the sky, and slopes littered with conifers and other dense stands of trees. Also, of fast-flowing white-water rivers. But, due to the darkness, the luminous green of the night-vision goggles was unable to give an appreciation of the landscape which had taken on a bland, two-dimensional look.

The team had touched down only minutes before and were now gathered together. Cunningham touched his talk button and said, "Eagle Nest, Delta One, radio check, over."

"Roger, Delta One, read you five by five."

"Copy, Eagle Nest. Delta Team down safe and moving toward the target. Out."

"Roger. Eagle Nest out."

Each member of Cunningham's team was carrying full kit and extra ammunition should it be required. He and Jeff Craig, along with Randall, carried suppressed CQBRs, while Hank Pullen had a suppressed M249 SAW.

Cunningham walked over to Craig and said, "You're on point. Take us north along the valley for three klicks until we hit the road."

"Copy, Boss," Craig said in a low voice and started forward into the darkness.

For the next two hours, they worked their way along the valley floor alongside the rushing water of a small river. At one point the narrow valley broadened to let another smaller, shallower stream in to join with the river.

The night was very cold, the air chilled enough that it pricked any exposed skin. Overhead in the clear night sky, there was a sliver of moonlight and a stunning profusion of millions of small stars. The going along the river was relatively flat, and for that, Cunningham was thankful, especially he looked around at the surrounding mountains and saw how rugged they seemed.

The team leader's comms came to life. "Delta One, we've reached Shaggy, over."

"Copy, Delta Two," Cunningham acknowledged. "Eagle Nest? Delta One, over."

"Copy, Delta One."

"We're passing Shaggy, moving to Daphne, over."

"Roger, Delta One. You're passing Shaggy."

Cunningham then said, "Delta Two, take us to Daphne."

"Copy."

Daphne was one more kilometer further along the road. They had two further waypoints to reach after that before attaining their target, designated Scooby. Cunningham was counting on them being in position before dawn so they could set up an observation post and be ready to infiltrate the fol-lowing evening. That was providing that everything went according to plan.

The Pentagon, Virginia

General Hank Jones was sitting behind his large desk when Kent Miller from the NSA entered. The big, gray-haired man looked up from the paperwork he was attending to and scowled. "What can I do for you, Kent? I take it that this isn't a social call?"

"I need you to rein your people in, Hank," Miller told him abruptly.

Placing his pen down on the polished desktop, Jones adjusted himself in his chair and asked, "What people might you be referring to? Perhaps you need to be a little more specific."

"Those hero commandos of yours who seem to have no regard for authority, and poke their noses into things which do not concern them."

"Does this have something to do with India?"

"It does. Someone is poking their noses into official NSA business."

Jones remained silent for a moment, his thoughts running rampant through his mind. Then he asked, "Is there a connection between India and the Pakistan thing?"

Miller sat down without being invited. "We believe so. The terrorists at the hotel in Jaipur were Pakistan SSG connected to Ajeet Khan, the man we believe is responsible for the theft of two nuclear weapons."

"I know about the weapons."

"Your people were flagged digging into files looking for information about a nuclear scientist named Javed Sharma."

Jones sat up a little straighter in his chair. "Go on."

"Apparently, he was at the hotel where your people were staying, and now he's disappeared. The leader of the force who assaulted the hotel, a man named Bawa, escaped and we believe he took Sharma with him."

"Which makes your mission into Kashmir doubly important."

"Yes. And I can't be distracted by incidents like the ones that your people are creating."

Jones nodded. "I'll fix it for you. Any word from your people on the ground?"

"They made their designated waypoint and will infiltrate tonight their time. There will be a real-time feed in the Situation Room if you care to swing by."

"I just might do that," Jones replied, knowing full well that he would be there.

Miller stood up. "Thanks, Hank. I appreciate you seeing me."

Kandahar, Afghanistan

The general picked up the encrypted satellite phone and said, "Thurston."

"What are you up to, Mary?" Hank Jones' voice asked from just over eleven thousand kilometers away.

"I don't know what you mean, sir."

"Come on, Mary. I just had Kent Miller from the NSA in my office."

"Then he would have told you what was going on then? Am I right, sir?"

"Yes. He said that your people, I'm assuming that it's our resident Bill Gates on your team, has been digging around looking into a nuclear scientist called Javed Sharma."

"Yes, sir. He's a nuclear scientist."

"I'm aware of that. But now I need you and your teams to stand down. The NSA has an operation ongoing in Kashmir and would appreciate it continuing without any interference. Understood?"

"Yes, sir. Can you tell me what?"

"Empty Quiver."

———————

"You are shitting me," Kane breathed. "This is about stolen nukes?"

Thurston nodded. "Let's just keep this between us for the time being, OK?"

Ferrero agreed. "Perhaps it's for the best."

"Who is leading the team in Kashmir?" Kane asked the general, rubbing his hands through his hair and scratching his head.

"I'm not sure. But it's only a recon mission. Get a look and report in."

"Why not SEALs?"

"Come on, Reaper. It's Kashmir. Why do you think?"

The team leader nodded. "Yeah, right. What are they going to do if they're found?"

"I don't know."

A silence descended over the small group. Then Kane asked, "What's up for us next?"

Thurston gave him a wicked grin, and her eyes seemed to sparkle as words formed in her mind. "You're going to love this. The Korengal Valley."

"Can I go home now?" Kane asked.

Thurston shook her head. "Not yet. Get the team together. Briefing will be in ten minutes."

"Yes, ma'am."

"OK, guys and gals, our next op is in the Korengal Valley," Thurston informed the group who had gathered quickly and were taking their seats in front of her.

Axe immediately put up his hand.

"What is it, Axel?"

He hesitated and glanced at Kane, who shrugged. The ex-Marine sniper didn't like it when she called him by his first name. It made him nervous. "I prefer not to go, ma'am. I've been there, and it wasn't nice at all."

"I've been there too," she replied.

Axe nodded and went quiet.

"As I was saying," her gaze focused on Axe before it diverted again. "The team is being sent into the Korengal Valley. In there somewhere, we are reliably informed, is a stockpile of illegal opium. Because the valley's main source of income is forestry, one of the local warlords thought it would be an ideal storage facility."

"How much are we talking about, ma'am?" Kane asked.

"Intel says maybe fifteen tons of the stuff stored there."

"What are we meant to do with it once we locate it?" Brick asked.

"Destroy it. Take some explosives with you and blow it," Thurston explained.

"How are we getting in?" Cara asked.

"The Night Stalkers have freed up a helo and are going to put you all in," Thurston elucidated. "Understand this. You will have no UAV cover nor will there be any QRF. There will be a couple of Apaches on standby, should you need them. But basically, you'll be on your own. It'll be a nighttime insertion, and all your weapons will be set up for silent running. Axe I suggest you pull a SAW from the armory."

"Yes, ma'am."

"There will be no satellite coverage, so you're going in blind. Reaper, this will be right up your line of expertise. Just watch your ass."

"Yes, ma'am."

CHAPTER SEVEN

Azad Kashmir

"Rick, we've got movement," Craig said, shaking him awake.

It was mid-afternoon, and the sun was still fairly high in the sky. Cunningham sat up and blinked his eyes to bring them into focus. After a moment, he reached out and grabbed his CQBR and asked his team-mate, "What kind of movement?"

"There are some Pakistani SSG men moving toward the foot of the slope," Craig explained. "They're shaping to come up this way."

Crouching low, Cunningham moved with quick steps to where Pullen sat observing the movements of the men below. From where the team had set up, the old Hydro Powerplant was perhaps six-hundred meters distant, but they were high enough up to have a clear view of it, which indicated that Khan had perhaps thirty men at his fingertips.

"They've stopped," Pullen said. "They're just at the foot of the slope."

Cunningham picked up his field glasses and swept the area. Everything appeared to be normal, yet he couldn't shake the feeling that it wasn't. "Wake Bo up."

They were operating in shifts of two. While he and Randall slept, Pullen and Craig were on watch. After two hours, they would swap, and it would be their turn to sleep. Bringing the glasses back to the men near the slope, he located four of them, standing about, talking.

Again, Cunningham swept the area and then stopped as he focused the glasses on the main turn-around at the front of the hydro station. "What happened to the guards at the turnaround?"

"They're still there," Pullen said, frowning.

"No, they're not."

The round whistled out of the afternoon and impacted Hank Pullen's head with a sickening thump. The operator dropped to the ground and didn't move.

"Contact!" Cunningham shouted. "Hank's down!"

The three men hugged the ground as a hailstorm of bullets snapped close over their heads, chopping leaves and branches from the surrounding brush and trees.

"Boss, how's Hank?" Jeff Craig called from where he lay. Craig was the unofficial team medic.

"Stay put, he's dead."

"Aw fuck!" Bo Randall snarled as he unleashed a torrent of fire along the face of the slope where the incoming fire had originated.

"Bo, get the SAW and put some extra fire on those bastards.

"Roger," the stocky man said, wriggling his way across to where the SAW was situated and took up the weapon. The suppressed machinegun rattled to life as the operator returned the incoming fire.

Cunningham pressed the button on his comms and shouted into the mic, "Eagle Nest, copy?"

Nothing

"Eagle Nest, this is Delta One. We are taking heavy fire, I say again, Delta Team is taking fire, over."

"Delta One? Eagle Nest. Say again your last."

A bullet kicked up dirt into Cunningham's face causing him to flinch. "Fuck. Eagle Nest, Delta team is taking fire. We have one team member down, over."

"Copy, Delta One," the voice came back calm, almost metallic. "Sitrep of you WIA?"

"WIA is KIA, Eagle Nest, copy?"

"Copy, Delta One."

"We're abandoning our position and starting our escape and evasion plan. Will make contact in one hour. Delta One out."

"Argh!" A pained cry drew Cunningham's attention. He looked and saw Craig laying on his back, looking at a wound to his upper arm.

"How is it?" the team leader called over.

"Flesh wound. Hurts like a bitch."

Cunningham pressed his talk button so Craig and Randall could hear him clearly. "Listen up, we're leaving. We'll move back across the slope and then up and over. You copy?"

"What about Hank?" Randall asked.

"Nothing we can do for him. We're going to have to leave Hank here."

There was a long silence from the other two operators, and Cunningham knew what they were thinking. They didn't like leaving anyone behind. Dead or alive. "Copy?"

Both voices came back, stoic in tone. "Copy."

"Move out."

Whitehouse Situation Room
Washington, DC

Normally the meeting would have involved the gathering of the full security council plus others. But President Jack Carter decided that would come later. Right now, he wanted just a few chosen people in at the start. The gray-haired sixty-seven-year-old was known to have a temper, and as he looked around the long table, it was obvious to those in the room that one of those explosive moods was simmering just below the surface.

"Fill me in on what we have," he growled.

Kent Miller hesitated by clearing his throat and then said, "Sir, we have a team in trouble in the field –"

"Be more specific, Kent, damn it," he said abruptly. "Where the hell are they?"

"Kashmir, sir."

Carter leaned forward, looked about the table. His eyes skirted over those who were there with him; Secretary of State, Frank Muir; Secretary of Defense, John Rolls; new CIA Director Melissa Smith; and Sam Weller in charge of Homeland Security. Plus, General Hank Jones and Rear-Admiral Alexander Joseph, the commander of the United States naval special warfare command (NAVSPECWARCOM).

Carter nodded. "The team that was sent in to find the stolen nuclear weapons?"

"Yes, sir."

"When did you last hear from them?"

"Three hours ago, after they were forced to withdraw from their position and escape and evade. They had one casualty at that time. KIA."

"Who?" asked Hank Jones.

"I'm not sure. Cunningham didn't say."

"Why am I just hearing about this now?" Carter growled, an edge to his voice.

Miller suddenly felt like a schoolboy being reprimanded in front of the class. "We were waiting for them to check-in, but they missed the time."

"Any word on the nukes?" Carter asked.

"No, sir."

"So, your team was discovered before they could find out if they were there or not?"

"Yes, sir."

"For fuck sake. There'd better be some good news?"

"Sorry, there is none. We believe that now it is known where they are hiding, that if the weapons are with them, then they'll certainly shift them."

It was Rear-Admiral Alexander Joseph who spoke next. The dark-haired man in the dress-whites said, "I can have a SEAL team in Kashmir within three or four hours, Mister President."

"No," John Rolls said hurriedly. "The last thing we want is American troops on the ground in Kashmir, pissing off the Indians and the Pakistanis. We've already had one fuckup this week."

Joseph knew he was referring to the UAV crashing in Pakistan.

"Then what are we going to do about our boys?" Joseph asked.

"They're on their own," Rolls said.

"Bullshit!" the rear-admiral snapped, leaning forward. "I'll not leave them there."

Hank Jones reached out and touched the angry man on the forearm. "Easy, Alex."

"We can't leave those boys out there, Hank."

"We're not going to," Jones reassured him.

"General," Miller said, "they knew the risks before they went in. They were told in no uncertain terms that if they were compromised in any way, they were on their own. No American armed forces would come for them."

"And none will," Rolls reiterated.

"I have a feeling that General Jones wasn't thinking of a conventional team like SEALS or Delta. Am I right, Hank?"

"That's right, Frank."

There was a derisive snort from Sam Weller, and Jones turned his withering gaze upon the bald man. "If you've got something to say, share. If not, shut the f—"

"OK," Carter interrupted. "We're not sending any American armed forces into Kashmir.

Rolls gave a nod of satisfaction. "Good."

"However," Carter continued, "I don't like the idea of leaving our boys hanging out to dry in some foreign country. Hank, tell me what you have in mind."

"Team Reaper, sir."

"They're not special forces, Mister President," Rolls pointed out.

"But they are led by the best-damned recon marine I've ever seen," Rear-Admiral Joseph said. "And they get things done."

"Fuck things up, more like," Weller muttered.

Carter shifted his gaze to Melissa Smith. "You're awfully quiet. I gave you the director's job at the CIA because you're opinionated and outspoken. I want your opinion now, Melissa."

Smith was tall and slim, with long black hair tied back in a ponytail. She was also the youngest in the room, being in her late thirties. "I think they should be allowed to try, sir. I know I wish I had Kane and his team. They'd be put to a lot better use than what they're being used for."

Carter stared at Jones and asked, "How long before you could have them on the ground?"

"Couple of hours, sir."

"How will you get them in?"

"I'll take care of that," came Joseph's reply.

Carter nodded. "All right then. You're up. Good luck."

Kandahar, Afghanistan

"Listen up!" Thurston's voice cut through the confused noise of the briefing room as the team tried to work out the reason for the mission suddenly being scrubbed.

They all quietened down and turned their attention toward their commander. The general continued. "We have a priority one situation that requires our immediate attention. However, this is for Reaper Team; it is volunteer only. I'll not order you to do it unless you are all comfortable with it."

"You'd better tell us what it is, ma'am, and we'll make that decision," Kane told her.

"Approximately five hours ago in Azad Kashmir, an NSA black ops team came into contact with some of our friends from India. The result of which is one operator dead, and three are MIA."

"Do we know who they are, ma'am?" Brick asked.

"Rick Cunningham's Delta Team."

"I know him. Good operator."

"Not if we don't find them."

"Why aren't SEALs going in?" Cara asked.

"The president has stipulated no US armed forces. I know this isn't what we necessarily do, but there are extenuating circumstances."

"Is this tied up with that other thing?" Kane asked.

Ferrero nodded. "Yes, it is."

"What other thing?" Arenas asked.

"The team were in Kashmir trying to locate a couple of stolen nukes."

"Do we have a two-part mission, General?" Kane asked.

"Yes. You need to locate Delta Team and have a look to see if the nukes have been moved. All the intel you need will be made available to you."

"In the middle of a nest of hornets."

"I didn't say it was going to be easy."

"Reaper," Axe said, "sounds like a recon mission to me."

Kane nodded then said, "Ma'am, if it's all the same to you, I'd like to make a captain's call on this one."

"Whoa, Reaper, what are you doing?" Cara asked, annoyed at the possibility of being overlooked.

"Axe is right. It's a recon mission. Too many of us downrange and we're more likely to get caught out. There's just two of us going. Axe and me."

"The hell you say!" Brick snapped.

"That's how it's going to be."

"And what if you guys –"

"Don't worry about us, Brickster." Axe gave him a huge shit-eating grin. "This is what we do."

Kane stared at Thurston. "Are you OK with this, ma'am?"

"Yes, that's fine. Sort out what you need."

Kane nodded and then said to Cara. "You and the others look over the intel while Axe and I kit up."

"OK."

The briefing broke up, and while Kane and Axe were getting their gear sorted, the others joined them with the intel and a laptop which Cara put on a small table after she'd cleared a space upon it.

"Before you all get started in on me," Kane said to them, "if I was you lot, I wouldn't be happy about it either. But the simple fact of it is, in this situation, two are just as good as five. And I picked Axe, not because I think he's better than any one of you, but because he's ex-recon like me. He's lived the life the same as me."

Cara looked grim but said, "I get it. We all do. But it doesn't mean we have to like it."

"Are we all good?" he asked, looking at every member individually.

They all nodded.

"OK, talk to me."

Cara hit a few buttons on the laptop and said, "Your LZ is here, approximately four klicks from this old hydro plant."

Kane finished with his body armor and looked at the screen. There was a plain topographical map on it as well as a satellite photo of the plant. Cara pointed at another point on the map and said, "This was Delta Team's OP."

"Good spot."

"Not good enough," she moved the screen. "This was their E and E route. But nothing has been heard from them since their last transmission. Word from their radio traffic had put around thirty tangos on the ground."

"What do you want us to do if this goes bad, Amigo?" Arenas asked.

"Nothing."

"Nothing?"

"Nothing. Brick plot us an E and E route."

"Gotcha."

Twenty minutes later, Cara approached Kane aside from the rest of the team. "Have you got everything you need?"

"I think so."

She held out one of the team's encrypted satellite phones. "Take this just in case your comms get screwed up."

"OK."

She started to fidget with his webbing and equipment. "You be careful out there."

He looked into her eyes and could see the concern. "Take care of everyone while I'm gone."

"They can take care of themselves. You, on the other hand, have an uncanny ability to get hip-deep in shit."

"Are you saying I attract trouble?" Kane asked with a smile.

"Bet your ass I am," Cara said. She turned to Axe. "You got that grenade you always carry?"

"More than one this trip, ma'am."

"See, even he knows how much attention you attract. Keep him safe, Axe."

"What about me?" he asked.

"You're like a bad smell. You always come back."

"And here I was thinking you actually liked me, Lieutenant."

Kane slapped him on the back. "She'll like you even less if you let something happen to me."

"What makes you so special?"

"I'm the Reaper."

"You suck."

They chuckled, and the light-hearted banter kept on for a few more minutes before Thurston appeared at the door. "Your taxi is waiting."

What she was referring to was a new UH-74 Stealth Hawk helicopter which Sikorsky had been working on for the past three years. But now after a few trials, it was about to be put into action for the first time. Thanks to Rear-Admiral Alexander Joseph.

The two team men started toward the door, and Brick yelled after them, "You two shitheads don't forget to duck."

Axe looked back over his shoulder and said, "I'll have mine deep-fried, along with a beer when we get back."

Azad, Kashmir

Adjeet Khan stopped the Havildar as he walked past. "Feroz, are the trucks ready?"

"They will not be long, Colonel," Bawa replied.

"And the Americans? Have they been found?"

"Not yet, sir."

"I want you to see to it personally."

"Yes, sir."

"Once you have taken care of the problem you can meet us in Boniyar."

"You can count on me."

"I always knew I could."

Headlights from one of the trucks flashed across them. Having been found so soon was a nuisance but not the end of it all. Khan had a backup plan which he was now putting into effect. Sharma was almost finished preparing the two suitcase devices when the Americans had been detected. After the shoot-out, Bawa had reported back to him that one of them had been killed; however, the other three were still on the run in the mountains behind the hydro plant.

Once complete, the weapons would be taken to their final destinations for detonation. Then the world would watch on helplessly as Pakistan and India finally did what they had been threatening to do for decades. Explode into nuclear war.

"Where is Professor Sharma?"

"He's over in the first truck. I have Deepak watching him."

Khan crossed to the vehicle, the soldier standing guard saluting him. The colonel opened the door and found Sharma sitting in the passenger seat. "How much longer will it take to finish your work?"

"Five or six hours."

"What about just one of them?"

"Half that time."

"When we arrive in Boniyar you will complete

the first one before moving onto the second. Understood?"

"Yes. Will you let me go once I am finished?"

"Of course. What else would I do? My fight is not with you."

Sharma seemed to be relieved at the news, foolishly taking the colonel at his word. Khan closed the door and said to Deepak, "Keep an eye on him when we arrive. Once he is finished, I want to look over them before I kill him."

"Yes, sir."

CHAPTER EIGHT

Azad, Kashmir

"Zero? Reaper One. We have eyes on the hydro plant. It looks pretty quiet."

"Copy, Reaper One."

Kane did a sweep with his field glasses once more, looking for any sign of life as the cold light of dawn started to filter along the river valley. There was a definite chill in the air which reminded him of the many winter mornings he'd experienced growing up. The tops of the ridges were orange in color from the early morning sunlight, while deep in the valley where they were, it was still a drab gray.

Two minutes later, Kane made the decision to infiltrate. "We're going in, Axe."

"Looks quiet enough, Reaper. My guess is that they've left the state."

"Mine too," Kane agreed. "Let's go."

They picked their way down the slope, moving between the trees and larger rocks, taking the time to place their feet carefully so as not to dislodge anything that would give away their presence. To some, it looked to be excruciatingly slow, but to Kane and Axe, it had once been a way of life. In one instance Kane could remember in Colombia where it took him eight hours to travel one kilometer.

The pair reached the foot of the slope and paused for a further five minutes. Axe was in front of Kane, and after the Team Reaper commander was sure that things were quiet, he reached out and squeezed Axe's shoulder.

They moved swiftly across the open ground to the first building where they sheltered against the wall. It was the smallest of those there and was made from sheets of iron.

Axe eased a look around the corner and then continued his move toward the largest of the buildings. The roar of the river grew steadily louder as the pair neared it. Axe drew up short of an open door and took up a position to one side. Kane stood on the other and eased his head around the corner. Everything looked clear.

With his suppressed 416 tucked into his shoulder, Kane moved around the corner of the jamb and into the building. He swept left while Axe came in behind him, sweeping right. It was like a big warehouse with steel girders in the roof and a vertiginous catwalk. In the center of the room was a secondary, hastily constructed box-like room. Not unlike a shipping container that had been sheared in half. While vigilant of their surrounds, the two men moved cautiously toward it.

They stopped just short, and Axe reached into Kane's rucksack and took out a small yellow, hand-held device. He switched it on and then watched as the numbers on the screen climbed.

Kane kept watch while he did it, his head on a swivel. Then once Axe was finished, he said, "We've got something, Reaper."

"Let's take a look inside."

Kane opened the door, and they peered into the darkroom. Apart from a table, some wiring scraps on top of it, and a few other odds and ends, the room was empty. "Check it, Axe before we step foot in there."

"Roger that."

Axe used the Geiger counter once more, and thirty seconds later, he said, "I wouldn't step in there unless you want to start glowing."

"Alright, let's close it up. It must be lead-lined."

After the door was closed, Kane said into his comms, "Zero, we've found nothing except a hot box, over."

"Copy. How hot?"

"Maybe someone would like to bury it for about ten thousand years hot."

"OK, Reaper. Get out of there, and we'll notify the general."

"Copy. We're going after Delta Team."

"Good luck. Zero, out."

Kandahar, Afghanistan

"Slick, find me those nukes," Ferrero snapped.

"On it," the red-headed tech said as his fingers danced across his keyboard.

"Look for trucks coming and going. It's the only way for them to transport everything they need."

Thurston appeared alongside her operations manager and looked at the large screen on the wall. Two red dots were starting to move across the screen toward the first line of the topographical map overlay.

"We need to inform the general about the hydro plant," Ferrero said.

"I'll get onto it," Thurston replied. "Where are they headed?"

"Up to Delta Teams OP."

Ferrero called back over his shoulder, "Someone bring up a map of the area for me. Set the parameters at one-hundred kilometers."

A new screen appeared before them, and Thurston and Ferrero looked on, studying it intently. "Khan could be anywhere in the region," the general stated.

"Can we task our satellite for a closer look at the roads leading out of the valley?" the operations leader called out to Swift.

"We can, but we'll lose track of our guys on the ground if we do, not that it makes much difference anyway. Right now, I'm running through images from the past twenty-four hours. We'll also lose our feed in around five minutes."

"Why?" asked Thurston testily.

"The satellite we're using is a flying dinosaur. I'm not even sure why it hasn't crashed back to earth yet."

"And that's the best you could do?" the general snapped.

"A man is only as good as his tools, ma'am. And right now, those tools are shit."

"Well fix it."

"I could see if the Ruskies have a bird in the vicinity. Maybe piggyback something off of that."

"Do it. I want eyes on our people at all times."

"What about the nukes?" Ferrero asked her. "Shouldn't they take precedence?"

"They will. Get Cara and Brick; I'm going to India."

Azad, Kashmir

"That's Hank Pullen," Kane said to Axe as they stared down at the corpse on the rocky ground.

"It don't seem right leaving him like this," Axe growled as he turned his gaze up the slope. "Are we going up?"

"Yes. We'll get to the top of the ridge and see what we find."

"Why does it have to be up?" Axe growled. "Next we'll be using ropes and fucking cams."

"Keep hold of that thought," Kane said, slapping him on the shoulder.

"Fuck you."

They reached the ridge an hour later where they stopped for a short break. Kane pressed the transmit button on his comms and said, "Delta One, copy?"

Static.

"Delta One, this is Reaper One, copy?"

Static.

Kane looked anxiously at Axe and then tried again. "Delta One, do you read, over?"

The comms crackled to life. "Copy, Reaper One."

Relieved, he asked, "What's your sitrep, Delta One?"

"Reaper One, Delta Team has two KIA, one WIA. We're holed up in a cave. Tangos all around our position. It's only a matter of time until they find us."

"Copy, Delta One. Send me your coordinates, over."

There was a pause in communications before Cunningham came back. "Are you on the ground, Reaper One?"

"Roger that. Now give me your coordinates."

The Delta Team leader rattled off the coordinates, and Kane acknowledged with, "Hold tight, Delta One, we'll get there as soon as we can. Reaper One out."

He turned to Axe who had retrieved and was studying a map. Kane hunched over it next to him and asked, "Where are they?"

"About four klicks east of here."

Kane nodded. "Zero, copy?'

"Reaper One? Bravo One, roger." It was Reynolds.

"Bravo One, we've made contact with Delta One. Moving to his location. Sending coordinates."

"Copy, Reaper One. I'll let Zero know. Out."

"All right, good buddy. Let's go and find our men and take them home."

———————

"Reaper," Axe whispered. "Tango close."

Kane froze in position twenty meters behind his friend. He noticed Axe had his 416 up to his shoulder in a firing position. "How many, Axe?"

"One. No, shit. There's three."

"I'm coming to you."

Kane eased his way forward to kneel beside Axe. "Where?"

Axe nodded toward a stand of trees where three men sat on a small outcrop of rocks. "They're just sitting there, waiting."

"Where there's some there's usually more."

Kane took his field glasses and scanned the area. He picked out an additional four scattered throughout the trees. "Seven so far."

"What do you want to do?"

"I don't see any chance of getting to Delta Team without cracking a few heads."

"Me neither."

"Or we can wait for dark."

"There is that."

"Better in the dark."

"Yes, it is."

———————

Jaipur, India

"The Indians aren't going to let us see their prisoner," Thurston growled to Cara and Brick. The hospital was busy, and two armed guards had been stationed outside the prisoner's room. "We need to get in there to talk to him."

"Don't they understand what's at stake?" Cara expressed her disbelief.

"I tried everything. But all they want to do is point fingers at Pakistan and talk tough. Stupid bastards. They have stolen nukes on their back doorstep, and they don't seem to want to know."

"So, what do we do?"

"We talk to him anyway."

"How are we going to do that, there's two guards with machine guns outside his door?" Cara asked.

"We'll need a distraction."

"I've got that covered," Brick said. "Just be ready.

Thurston frowned. "What are you going to do?"

He gave her a wry smile. "Create a diversion. Just be ready."

He disappeared around the corner and walked up to the two guards. He stared at them before saying, "I need to go in there."

Both uniformed men returned his stare but said nothing.

"You heard me, right?" Brick asked.

Again, there was no response.

The ex-SEAL shrugged his shoulders and made to push through between them. The two guards immediately moved to block his path. But Brick wasn't about to be stopped. He pressed forward and caused the guards to exert more force.

He stepped back to gather himself and then pushed forward again. This time the Indian guards had had enough. They started yelling at the American and forcing him back. Brick appeared to relent and allowed himself to be steered along the hospital hallway away from their post a short distance.

Keeping watch on the situation from around the corner, Thurston and Cara waited until the doorway was clear and then hurried forward together, slipping into the room and silently pulling the door closed behind them.

Inside the room, a hard hospital bed held their target, who was lying handcuffed to the metal rail by his left wrist. He had an IV line hooked into the crook of his elbow, with tape holding the canula to his hairy arm, and a heart monitor attached by what looked to be a jumble of various colored wires.

Awake but not alert, the man turned his head sluggishly to see who had entered his room, a confused look washing over his visage. "Who are you?" he asked with a dry-throated rasp.

Thurston walked across to his bedside and stared down at him. "Listen to me very closely. I don't have much time, so I will ask questions, and you will answer them. Got it?"

With realization dawning on him that these visitors were here without authority and shouldn't be in his room, he opened his mouth to cry out. The general's hand clamped firmly over his mouth, stifling the shout. Thurston brought her face to within an inch of his, a menacing sneer on her face, and whispered harshly, "Listen up, motherfucker. I have no time to piss around with you. Understood? Now, where was Khan taking the nuclear weapons?"

Recognition and fear flooded the man's eyes. Thurston took her hand away to allow him to answer, but once again, the man opened his mouth to shout. The general, totally expecting such a reaction, dropped her elbow into his midsection, forcing all the air from his lungs. The Pakistani tried to cry out in pain, but with the absence of air in his lungs, he failed to emit a sound.

Thurston leaned in close again and said, "Next time I'll break your neck, asshole. Now, the nuclear weapons?"

Allowing him to take a breath, the general pushed the man's head back against the pillow where he opened his mouth and said, "The hydro station."

"Nope, he left there because he was found. Where's his backup?"

"Boniyar."

"As in Kashmir, Boniyar?"

"Yes."

"What are his targets?"

Nothing.

Moving her hands quickly, Thurston clamped one over his mouth once more, and the other groped around under his hospital gown until she found his nipple beneath it and grasped it with two fingers. Then she gave it a savage twist, causing him to arch his back.

Beads of sweat appeared on his forehead as his muted screams failed to get past Thurston's hand. She looked at him with a stern expression and hissed, "Imagine what having a fucking baby feels like. Now, what does he plan to do with the weapons?"

The Pakistani blurted something out from behind her hand, and she took it away so he could repeat
what he had said. "He plans to make two weapons to
go in a box."

"A box?"

The man nodded vigorously, unwilling to have
her deliver more pain. "Yes."

"What kind of box?" Thurston snapped.

"One with a handle."

The general looked at Cara, who was watching the doorway. She frowned at Thurston, who
shrugged her shoulders in return. The man added,
"One you can put your clothes in."

"A suitcase?" the general asked hurriedly.

"Yes, yes. A suitcase."

"He's putting together two suitcase bombs?"

The man nodded. "Yes."

"We have to get out of here, Ma'am," Cara said
urgently.

"I still have questions."

"Sorry, but you're out of time."

"Damn it."

Thurston hurried over to the door but was forced
back by Cara. "Not that way."

Cara's eyes darted around the room, and all that
she saw was the window. As she hurried over to it,
she hoped against all hope that it wasn't a sealed unit
like most hospital windows.

It was.

"Shit."

The two women turned and looked at each other and then at the door as it slowly opened.

Within the space of a couple of heartbeats, two things happened. Cara hurried across to stand behind the door, and Mary Thurston took off her T-shirt to reveal a black lace bra which pushed her breasts up and accentuated her cleavage.

The door finished its swing and then nothing. Cara watched as the expression on Thurston's face changed, and then a voice said, "Now there's a sight you don't see every day."

Thurston rolled her eyes and reached down for her T-shirt. "What are you doing here?"

"Something happened, and the guys walked right past without stopping."

"Well, let's get out of here, shall we?"

The three of them slipped out the door and into the hallway. No sooner had they exited the room when the man inside began to scream. Traynor smiled at Thurston. "Sounds like he was enjoying the show."

"Shut up."

Azad, Kashmir

The cave mouth looked like a black hole in the middle of the green haze. Kane edged forward cautiously, ducking under a low tree branch. Behind him, Axe swept to their rear and the left as he kept rear security. So far, they had managed to slip past all the searchers.

As he neared the gaping maw of the cave, Kane whispered, "Delta One?"

The sound of a flurry of activity emerged from inside the cavern, and a voice came back, "Reaper One?"

"That's us."

Kane saw the figure appear at the cave mouth and he and Axe moved forward. "We're coming in."

Once inside, Cunningham said, "Glad to see you guys."

"Glad you're alive to see us," Kane responded. "Is your WIA mobile?"

"I'm mobile," Jeff Craig answered from further back in the cave.

"That's Craig, he's my number two."

Kane nodded. "The other guy with me is Axe. He's a pain in the ass."

"Shit," Axe hissed. "No wonder I have trouble finding friends."

There was a light chuckle before Cunningham asked, "How'd you manage to get through?"

"Us recon marines can do anything," Axe told him with a huge grin.

"I'm sorry about your guys," Kane said on a more somber note.

"Yeah, me too. They were good men."

Kane pressed his talk button on his comms and said, "Zero? Reaper One, copy?"

He was met with static.

"The comms are shit in this part of the valley," Cunningham said. "Can't get anything out because of the mountains."

"Then we'll just have to do without them for the time being," Kane said. "How're you guys off for weapons and ammo?"

"We've got some."

"Let's go. Axe you do rear security. We'll get out of here and head up. Understood?"

They all agreed and then walked toward the mouth of the cave.

———

Bullets ricocheted from the granite rock face about ten yards from the cave mouth. Kane brought up his suppressed 416 and squeezed off two well-placed shots. The laser sight had landed on the chest of a Pakistani shooter a heartbeat before they were fired. The man jerked and fell to the ground.

Kane swept left and through the green haze of his NVGs found another target and fired again with the same result. "Axe, sweep right."

"All clear, Reaper."

"OK, keep moving before we –"

The night was ripped apart by automatic gunfire from the slope above the cave. Kane could feel the earth tremble with the impacts of the bullets. "Axe take them left, I'll catch up," Kane snapped as he unloaded the rest of his magazine at the position from which the fire was coming.

Dropping out the empty magazine, Kane slapped home a fresh one and began to fire once again. Still, the fire came down from above, but he figured there to be only one man. Still, one man with a machine gun could keep him pinned down long enough for others to join him.

Kane took a grenade from his webbing and pulled the pin. He let the spoon fly, counted a couple of beats, and then threw it up the slope. With a loud roar and a flash of orange, the thing detonated, sending out scything metal shards. The machine gun fell silent, and Kane was soon on the tail of the others.

For the next twenty minutes, the four men worked their way along the valley back toward the hydro station. Kane called a halt, and they gathered their breath and listened for any danger. The only noise seemed to be coming from behind them, so once more they pressed on, Kane leading them up the slope toward higher ground.

An hour later, Kane stopped them once more and tried his comms. "Zero, copy?"

"Copy, Reaper One. Good to hear your voice."

"Zero we need immediate extract."

"Wait one."

"Axe, how are we looking?"

"All good so far, Reaper."

"How are you two?" he then asked Cunningham.

"We're good."

Ferrero's voice came back over the comms. "Reaper One, you're down for an extract at oh-seven hundred. You're to climb to the top of a ridge and then send your coordinates for a Stabo extract. Over."

"Copy. Out."

"Well, let's keep climbing."

———————

Boniyar, Kashmir

"They got away," Bawa told Khan.

Khan's stare was cold. "What do you mean?"

"We managed to kill one more, but the others hid. They received some help from outside sources and were lifted out by helicopter this morning. We saw them being extracted from a ridge."

"That is inconvenient."

"They do not know where we are."

"And we will be gone before they find this place," Khan said. "The packages are ready."

"When are we leaving?" Bawa asked.

"Tonight. Take five men with you to make sure you are not interrupted in any way. I will take the others with me. Be ready."

"Yes, sir."

Bawa left, and a man emerged from another, smaller room. Khan turned to face him as the man asked, "Is there a problem?"

Khan shook his head. "Nothing to speak of. It is too late to stop us now."

The man narrowed his already narrow eyes. "Are you sure?"

"You worry too much Jin Zhāng," Khan said. "When dark arrives, we will all be on our way. And within the week, southern and central Asia will be ablaze."

"Tell me why you have turned against your country?"

"My country?" Khan spat. "My country is weak. It bows down to the imperialist Americans without pride. When China sweeps south with its massive armies, the government will know what true power is."

"And India?" Zhāng asked.

"I needed them for the plan to work," Khan explained. "But what about you?"

The Chinese billionaire nodded. "The government has over one million of my people locked up in re-education camps. Someone needs to make a statement for them."

Khan stared at Zhāng. "You are Muslim?"

"Yes."

"Who would have figured that? I guess we all

have our reasons for doing what we are. But you realize what your statement will do?"

"It will draw China into a war which the rest of the world will not be able to stay out of. China may have the troops, but it lacks air and sea superiority. However, there is something else that will make it all possible."

"Which is?"

"For the past five years, my electronics company has been supplying the PRC with new guidance systems for all of its weapons which have been upgraded across its stocks. Even its nuclear weapons have them. When the war starts, a code will be triggered, and all of China's systems will be rendered useless. Even their planes will fall from the sky. But to make it happen, we need a war. You have supplied a means to an end."

Khan was suddenly angry. His plan had counted on the PRC troops swarming across the frontier. "But my plan –"

"Your plan will still work," Zhāng cut him off. "For me."

Suddenly a handgun appeared in the Chinese billionaire's hand. Khan was stunned. He looked down at the weapon and then back to Zhāng. "My men will kill you," the SSG commander pointed out as though the man who was about to kill him had forgotten that important factor.

Zhāng shrugged his shoulders, and a wan smile

split his aged face. "No, they won't. Money is such a powerful motivator."

Without another word, the Chinese billionaire shot Khan dead.

"It is done," said Bawa.

"Yes. Do you have someone to take the other package to Pakistan?"

Bawa nodded.

"I will make sure the money has arrived in all of the bank accounts before tomorrow morning."

CHAPTER NINE

Boniyar, Kashmir

Captain Javed Mishra of the Indian 9th Para Special Forces signaled his men forward toward the building identified as their target in Boniyar. He led a team of twenty men, split into three sub-teams. One team each would cover the left and right flanks while the section he led would take the middle. They moved with swift, sure strides, their Tavor TAR-21 Bullpup assault rifles up in the firing position.

Mishra could hear the beat of his heart in his ears as he rushed forward. Out of the corners of his eyes, he saw the two other teams break cover and move rapidly forward. Back behind him, still in the ditch that they'd used to infiltrate close enough to storm the target building were the two nuclear specialists and bomb disposal techs who would go to work after the areas were secure.

Voices erupted over Mishra's headset as the two separate teams breached the large building. One was reporting that the building was empty. The other a body. Then a third voice, this one more frantic. Something about a trap and a bomb and –

Kandahar, Afghanistan

The big screen was a constant news feed of Indian and Pakistani Forces flowing into Kashmir just south of Jammu, and the ensuing battles. On the ground and in the air. Reports coming out of the region were of heavy losses on both sides, and it had only been two days since the nuclear explosion that had kicked it all off.

Both India and Pakistan had all available troops along their frontier stand to, and China was moving at least two divisions to its own border with the disputed region in preparation for the possibility of it spilling over.

Even America and Great Britain, while calling for a halt in hostilities, had mobilized their own forces and were flying troops to Afghanistan to be on standby. Both SEALs and SAS were dropped covertly into Kashmir as soon as the fighting started, to observe the proceedings.

And as the team watched on, Airforce One was

winging its way across the Pacific to talks in New Delhi.

"This is just one big fuckup," Axe said aloud.

Cara nodded. "Let's hope that it can be stopped before it goes much further. It's scary stuff, especially because they both have nukes. Thank God it wasn't a full-blown warhead."

Brick turned and looked at Ferrero, who stood with his arms folded, watching the feed. The operations leader said nothing, just looked on stoically. The ex-SEAL said, "Any news of Khan?"

Ferrero shook his head. "Nothing."

"They wouldn't really go nuclear, would they?" Reynolds asked.

"They've been threatening to do it to each other for a long time now," Ferrero said. "Each blames the other for what happened, and Pakistan isn't about to lose face by admitting that one of their own stole two nuclear weapons and disappeared with them."

Suddenly Kane appeared, a concerned expression upon his face. "Operations, now."

The team followed him into operations and were surprised to find SEAL Chief Borden Hunt, code-named Scimitar and three others there with him.

Two of those with Hunt, they'd worked on a previous mission with. Mike Oil was Hunt's sniper, a tall, thin man with brown eyes. Next to him stood Rucker, the team combat medic. The third man was a newcomer, at least to the team anyway. He was a solidly built man with tattoos on his arms, a goatee beard, and close shaved head.

"Well if it ain't our friendly neighborhood squids," Axe said with a smile.

Hunt smiled. "Howdy, Axe. My sister has been trying to call you."

Axe looked shocked as all eyes turned toward him, looking for an answer. Hunt chuckled, and they all realized that he was joking.

"What brings you to our lovely patch of desert?" Cara asked.

"It seems you guys have kicked a hornet's nest," Hunt explained. "But the Admiral will tell you what's happening."

"Who's your friend?" Reynolds asked.

"Gunner Jenkins."

Rear-Admiral Alexander Joseph walked into the room accompanied by General Thurston. They stopped in front of the group and paused for several moments while everyone took their seats. It was Thurston who spoke first. "OK, listen closely. For those of you who don't know, this is Rear Admiral Alexander Joseph from Special Warfare Command."

The Admiral nodded and stepped forward. "There have been a few new developments with our search for –"

He stopped when another man entered the room. This one they all knew. General Hank Jones. The first thought through everyone's minds when they saw him was, *Fuck this must be ba*.

"Sorry to interrupt, Joe. Continue."

"As I was saying, there have been a few new developments." He stepped aside, and the large screen came on. "What you are seeing is the target building in Kashmir when Khan and his people supposedly split up."

They all watched the satellite picture and saw three vehicles leave the area of the building that Khan had used to finish his work with the nuclear weapons. "We assumed that Khan was in one of these SUVs," Joseph continued. "But voice analysis from recordings before the weapon detonated leads us to believe that Khan was killed on site. An hour later, the SUVs split up. One vehicle headed for Pakistan, the second for India."

"They really mean to get this party fired up," Axe said, not taking his eyes from the screen.

"It would seem so. And what better place to start it?"

"Why would they kill Khan?" Cara asked.

"We don't know the answer to that."

"I'm not too concerned about the known," Kane said. "What about the unknown? Where the hell is that third vehicle headed and what or who is in it?"

"China," this came from Hank Jones.

A sudden heavy silence descended upon the room. Grim expressions on every face.

"Are you certain, sir?" Kane asked.

"Reasonably," Jones said. "We scoured everything we could and came up with this man."

The picture changed, and Zhāng appeared on the screen. "This is Jin Zhāng, Chinese billionaire."

"What would he want with a nuclear weapon?" Brick asked.

"He's Muslim. Not many people know it, but he is. And with all that China is doing with its re-education program, it's not really surprising."

"So, what you are saying is that he means to detonate it on Chinese soil."

"We believe so, yes."

"Have you told the Chinese this?"

"No."

"Why the hell not?"

"It's complicated, and you don't need to know."

"So why are you telling us this?" Kane asked, afraid he already knew the answer.

Joseph took over the dialogue. "Everyone here is being split up into three teams. Three teams, three nuclear devices."

"Who's the lucky pricks that are going to China?" Axe asked jokingly.

When his words were met with silence, he cursed in a low voice.

"Scimitar and his team get that job," Joseph explained.

Kane stared at the SEAL team leader and saw the stoic expression on his face. Then he asked, "Why us?

Why not use your own guys, Admiral?"

"Most of our special forces are deployed across the globe or are on standby in case this thing goes further south than where we're happy for it to be. Plus, you people get the job done no matter what. And right at this time, that attitude is what we need. No rules of engagement. You just head downrange and get it done by any means necessary."

"What's the plan?"

"You'll head into Pakistan and stop the device at all cost. General Thurston will take another team to India."

"What support do we get?"

"Everything that you need," Jones said adamantly.

"What about Scimitar?"

"Chief Hunt knows the score on that one."

"In other words, if he gets into trouble, he'll have his cock dangling in the wind," Kane snapped.

"Reaper," Thurston cautioned his outburst.

"It's Chinese sovereign territory, Reaper," Jones said. "You know how things are."

"So, let them sort it out."

"Let it go, Reaper," Hunt said quietly. "We've got this."

"You sure?"

"Yeah."

"Now that we have that settled, shall we get back to the task at hand?" Joseph asked abruptly.

When no one said anything, he carried on. "It is

up to us to neutralize the threat because if either the Pakistanis or Indians, especially the Indians, find out that these weapons are on their soil then things will go from bad to shit real fast."

"What do we do when we find them?" Kane asked.

"Secure the weapons until we can get them out of there."

"This should be fun," Axe growled.

Lahore, Pakistan

"You and your big fucking mouth," Kane growled as more bullets whined overhead punching huge holes in the air.

"How did I know there would be a fifty cal. I mean fuck, this is Lahore," Axe shot back.

"They have a damned nuke, Axe. Why wouldn't they have a fifty? Eleven million people in the city and I'm stuck behind this thing with you."

"You can leave any time you want. And just so you know, these ain't the same assholes."

"Whatever."

The SUV they were hidden behind rocked violently as another round smashed into the engine block.

"You ladies finished bitching over there?" Cara

asked from where she, Brick, and Arenas were hiding in a garbage choked alley.

"Cara, can you get a shot at this son of a bitch?"
Kane asked over his comms.

"I have an M17, Reaper. Someone told us we
couldn't bring out heavier weapons on this op. Remember?"

"Improvise, Reaper Two."

Cara leaned around the corner of the alley mouth
and raised her right hand, extending her middle finger at the shooter. "Hey! Fuck you!"

She lurched back as even more, heavy-caliber
bullets chewed large chunks of concrete from the
corner of the building's façade. "Don't think that
worked, Reaper."

Kane shook his head. "I'm surrounded by come-
dians."

After Swift had managed to track the Pakistan
suitcase nuke to Lahore, Kane and his team were
inserted to intercept. Which brought them to where
they were. A now deserted street, lined with close-
built buildings not unlike a concrete canyon.

They had stopped the truck which was now
transporting the suitcase and killed the driver
and passenger, along with the three escorts in the
back. But then the technical with the fifty-caliber
appeared from nowhere and had driven them back,
leaving the truck and nuclear device in the middle of
no man's land.

Kane said into his comms, "Zero, do we know who these pricks are?"

"They're not SSG, Reaper One."

"I can see that."

A burst of small arms fire echoed along the street, punctuating the heavier boom of the fifty. This time the SUV sounded as though it was getting peppered by hailstones rather than giant boulders.

"Reaper One, there's movement on the rooftops to your two o'clock, and we have indications of several police vehicles headed your way."

A fifty caliber round blew through the SUV and exited between Kane and Axe before punching into an abandoned tuk-tuk.

"How many of these guys are there, Bravo Four?"

"All up, seven or eight," Swift said. "Maybe even ten. It's hard to tell."

The sounds of sirens grew loud as two Pakistani police cars arrived and came to a stop further along the street. The appearance of those vehicles drew fire like moths to a flame. Which was directly both good and bad.

Bad because within moments of their arrival, both teams of law enforcement officers and their vehicles were torn apart by gunfire. The distraction was good for Kane and Axe who exploited the opportunity to break cover and head for the alley in which the others sheltered.

"Come on," Kane growled and started running

across the street.

Both men covered the distance in record time as chunks of asphalt began to lift behind them. They reached the alley and instantly pressed their backs against the wall, taking a moment to regain their breath. Brick smiled at them both. "Your friends out there aren't very nice, are they?"

"Fuck you," Axe panted.

Cara leaned out and fired at a shooter on a rooftop across the street. She saw the bullet strikes on the parapet before she ducked back with a soft curse. "Might as well throw rocks at them for all the good it's doing. What I'd give to have my one-ten about now."

Arenas stared at Kane. "You are the boss, *Amigo*. What do you suggest we do?"

"We have to get to the truck to get the suitcase."

"Perhaps that is a little easier said than done."

As though having an epiphany, Axe suddenly chimed in with, "I have an idea."

"What?" The word came in unison as they looked at each other.

He gave them all a weird smile and said, "You'll see. Hold my beer."

"Oh, shit," Kane muttered.

"What?" asked Cara. "Why do I get the feeling that this is going to be bad?"

Axe tucked the M17 into his jeans and, with an efficiency of movement, crossed to a perpendicular downpipe coming from the rooftop above. Grasping it he gave it a shake, assessing its suitability, shrugged, and immediately began to climb.

"What the hell?" Brick muttered.

Axe had the appearance of a monkey scampering up a tree. Momentarily, he had reached the top and was onto the roof. He hurried across to the front and crouched behind a balustrade.

"Reaper, copy?"

"Copy."

"You see along the street a piece where that transformer is on the phone pole?"

After a few moments, Kane came back. "Yes."

"Shoot it for me?"

"What?"

"Just shoot it."

"OK, give me a minute."

A flurry of gunshots erupted from below and within seconds, the transformer blew with a loud bang and a shower of blue and orange sparks. "Thanks."

"What are you doing, Axe?"

But the ex-recon marine sniper didn't answer. Instead, he removed the belt from around his waist, leaned down over the edge of the building to where a power line came in, and then, like a crazy man, jumped from the rooftop out into thin air.

"Holy shit!" Brick exclaimed. "You see that?"

Kane looked up and shook his head. "Crazy asshole. Give him some cover fire–don't bother."

As they all watched Axe and his death-defying flyover, the line at the other end gave way, and he fell to the street below like a buzzard with its wings clipped. Kane winced as the big man hit hard, and had it not been for the noise of the gunfire; he was sure they would have heard the impact.

"Well," said Cara, "he's not James Bond. Shit. Cover me."

Cara broke away from the alley swiftly, while behind her, the rest of the team sprayed bullets at everything that resembled the enemy. She reached Axe and grabbed his shirt collar. Using all her strength, she began to haul him out of the street. "Are you OK?" she panted from the exertion.

He moaned. "I sure can't fucking fly."

"I've seen you do some dumb shit, but this was one of your best," Cara growled as bullets started kicking up around her feet.

She managed to get the stunned Axe to the scant cover of a small car's front end on the opposite side of the street before dropping to her knees and straddling him. "Trust me to pick the smallest car in the fucking street."

"I don't think we have time for this right now, ma'am," Axe managed to get out, swallowing hard.

"Shut up, or I'll shoot you," Cara growled.

"Is he OK?" Kane asked over the comms.

"More than OK, I'd say," Cara shot back. "But now

I'm pinned down with Casanova here."

"Hey, you're the one on top," Axe pointed out.

"Reaper One, I can see movement from the tangos. It looks like they're making a move for the truck."

"Can't do much, Zero, especially while they've got that fifty still operating."

There was a long pause before Ferrero said, "Get out of there, Reaper One. I'm calling it. You need to regroup, and we'll work out what to do from there."

"Cara, did you get that?" Kane asked her.

Bullets peppered the small car, wrecking the panels and annihilating any intact glass, causing Cara to duck low, almost burying her face into Axe's throat. "I heard. But tell me where I'm supposed to go."

"Good question," Axe said. "But I think I might have an idea."

"Oh, no, not another one. It was your last brilliant idea that put us here in the first place."

Axe ignored the jibe and said, "Get out of here, Reaper. We'll meet up with you after we extricate ourselves from this romantic embrace."

"Jesus Christ," Cara muttered.

"Are you sure, Axe?"

"We got this, Reaper."

"OK. We're pulling back."

Another flurry of gunfire was punctuated by the louder noise of the fifty-caliber. The small car rocked violently, more glass spraying across the hood and down onto Cara and Axe.

"All right, Einstein, what now?"

Axe pointed at an undamaged pane of window glass in the building next to their position. "That way."

Cara shook her head. "Nope. Not dressed like this, sweet cheeks."

She was wearing jeans and a blue singlet top. While it was suitable attire for most activities, crashing through a glass barrier wasn't on the list and was one of the last things she wanted to do. Whereas Axe was wearing a T-shirt.

Without so much as a thought, he dropped his gaze, running an appreciative look over her semi-exposed cleavage. He grinned and nodded. "I can see your problem."

She cuffed him across the top of his head. "Asshole."

"OK, ma'am, as pleasurable as it is, you're going to have to get off me so I can make an opening for us."

Cara rolled to the side, presenting as small a target as she could. Axe wriggled up onto his knees and sucked in a couple of deep breaths. His steely gaze settled on the window and then psyching himself up for the impact, he lurched to his feet with a grunt of pain and ran straight at his target.

The M17 came up in Axe's hand, and he fired twice, shattering the glass. It fell away in splintered shards before he reached it, the obstruction clear by the time he launched himself through the opening.

With a shake of her head, Cara said, "Shit." Then she too clambered to her feet and followed Axe through the opening.

———————

"Shall I send someone after them?" Madina Umarov asked with more than a hint of excitement as she replaced an empty magazine in her FN F2000 Bullpup.

Ibragim Barayev looked at her thoughtfully before shaking his head. "No. Let us get what we came for."

Madina nodded. The raven-haired Chechen beauty had been with Barayev for three years. They'd fought side-by-side on more than one occasion, and now, here in Pakistan, their dreams were about to be realized with the acquisition of a nuclear weapon. She stepped in close to him and reached up, pulling his face down toward hers. She kissed him passionately before pulling back, giving him a seductive smile.

A smile split the big, broad-shouldered terrorist's face. "Go."

He watched her lithe form hurry away from him as she barked orders. Barayev turned away and called out to one of his men. "Shamil!"

A thin man carrying another F2000 ran over to him. "Get everyone ready to leave."

The man named Shamil spoke into a radio, and within moments three SUVs arrived. Barayev turned to look for Madina and saw her heading in his direction, holding a silver suitcase and being escorted by three of their men. "Put it in the back of our vehicle, and we will leave."

While his men formed a compact perimeter, Barayev helped Madina put their prized possession into the rear of the SUV. Once it was done, the perimeter collapsed, and they all climbed aboard the vehicles and drove off.

———

Kandahar, Afghanistan

"Someone get me Jones on the line," Ferrero snapped as he watched the SUVs drive away. Then to Swift, "Slick, can we stay on them?"

"I'll do my best."

"OK, someone tell me who these people were. If you don't know, find out. They knew about the weapons just like we did, and were well prepared to take them."

Reynolds called across to Ferrero, "The general is on line one, Luis."

He picked up the phone and hit the button. "Sir."

"What's happened, Luis?"

"There was a third team at the intercept point,

General."

"Who?" Jones asked, and Ferrero could hear the hard edge to his voice.

"We're not sure, sir, but they knew about the device just like we did."

"Did Kane and his team secure it?"

"No, sir, they were outgunned and didn't have a chance."

"Damn it. So, what is happening now?"

"We're trying to keep track of the new players and where they're headed. Also, I've got my people trying to find out who they are."

"And Kane?"

"I'll direct him to a safehouse until we work out what the hell is going on."

"All right, keep me apprised."

"Yes, sir."

Jones hung up, and Ferrero did the same.

"Luis?"

He turned and saw Reynolds waving to him. He walked over to her work station, and she said, "General Thurston is about to intercept her suitcase nuke."

"Let's hope this goes better than the last one."

CHAPTER TEN

Chandigarh, India

The wide street had a line of Chakrasiya trees on one side and light poles on the other. Back in the trees, Thurston could make out the rundown, red-painted building. As they drove along, she was certain that they would have missed it had it not been for the benefit of their outside help.

"How many are inside?" Thurston asked through her comms.

"We think five, ma'am," Swift said.

"They're all armed, I take it?"

"Yes, ma'am."

The general turned her gaze to her two companions in the SUV with her. Teller and Traynor studied the building through the trees too. A lone sentry had been posted at the front near the truck they had switched to so as not to draw attention. He walked back and forth in short strides, his pace nonstop.

Traynor checked the loads in her M17 and asked, "What do you want to do, ma'am?"

"Luis, is there any indication as to what their target might be?"

"Not yet. Mind you, with a nuclear device you don't exactly have to be on top of a target to blow it up."

"True."

"We've got movement," Teller said, passing the field glasses to his commander.

Thurston took them and placed them up to her eyes. Two more men had appeared and were talking with the sentry. Recognition of one of the men bloomed right away, and the general said, "Well now, we meet again."

"Ma'am?" Traynor said.

"My old friend Feroz Bawa is here. It looks like he's in charge."

"Do we go?"

Bawa turned away and walked back inside, leaving the other two men standing near the truck. Thurston quickly took her weapon from Traynor and expertly attached a suppressor to it, nodding. "Yes, let's do it."

The two SSG men seemed surprised when the black

SUV appeared suddenly and screeched to a halt. They began moving their weapons up as the doors to the vehicle opened and two people, a man and a woman, climbed out, a third person remaining with the vehicle.

Before they had the chance to depress the triggers on their weapons, the suppressed M17 spat fire, punching bullets into their chests and they performed a macabre death dance, jerking briefly before slumping to the ground, the weapons spilling from their grasp. Traynor and Thurston stood over them momentarily long enough to put a bullet in their heads.

Behind them Teller came out of the SUV, his own weapon up and ready to use. With hand signals, Thurston directed them both toward the scarred door, which would allow them access to the interior.

The building was big without being huge. It was double story and had large windows along the second floor. While Teller and Traynor moved toward the door, Thurston lagged behind where she could cover the windows above. Just in case.

Traynor and Teller stopped either side of the door, got set, and then breached.

Apart from a single round table in the center of the space, which held the open suitcase, with three men staring at it, the room had been stripped bare long ago. It retained a musty smell, one which had built up after years of being sealed within.

The three men grasped at their weapons; the surprise obvious on Bawa's face. The suppressed M17s in Teller and Traynor's hands coughed loudly in the enclosed area. Two of Bawa's men jerked briefly before falling to the stained floor.

The Havildar managed to get off a wild shot before being brought down by two bullets to his chest.

Teller and Traynor moved forward quickly, sweeping the room as they went. Behind them came Thurston who strode purposefully toward the table. She checked inside the suitcase and was relieved to see the digital display in a state of darkness. She said into her comms, "Zero, this is Bravo, copy?"

Instead of Ferrero's voice filling her head, all that the general could hear was static. She frowned. "Zero, this is Bravo, copy?"

She glanced at Traynor and shook her head.

"Zero, this is Bravo Two, copy?" Traynor tried, with the same result. He shook his head. "Nothing, ma'am."

"Are we being jammed?"

"Good possibility."

"Shit," she cursed out loud and ran toward the entrance they had just utilized.

Thurston glanced out through the opening to see two Mercedes SUVs coming to an abrupt stop next to their own vehicle, disgorging eight fully-armed men in tactical gear, making her blood run cold.

Kandahar, Afghanistan

"What do you mean we've lost everything?" Ferrero growled. "Get it back up!"

"I'm trying, but we're being jammed."

"I don't give a shit what they're doing, just what you are. Fix it."

"Yes, sir."

Ferrero reached for the satellite phone and punched in a number he had committed to memory. He heard the line buzz for two rings before being picked up at the other end by a sleep-addled voice that said, "Miller."

"What the fuck have you got us into?"

"What? Ferrero?" The NSA man was confused, sitting up groggily and rubbing his face.

"Yeah, it's me."

"Do you realize–"

"Shut up and listen," Ferrero snapped. "In the past couple of hours, while you've been sleeping, another player has joined our little game. They've taken the Pakistan device, and I've just lost all feed with my India team. You need to drag your ass out of that nice warm bed and find out what the fuck is going on before everything gets fucked up even further."

"What do you mean?"

"I'll have someone send what we have to your office. Now, get moving."

Ferrero hung up. He could feel the vein at his

temple start to throb as his ire blossomed into a rage. He took several deep breaths to calm and bring himself back into control, then turned toward Swift. "Give me some good news, Slick."

———————

Chandigarh, India

"We've got incoming," Thurston called back over her shoulder as she fired two shots at the attackers before they could make a move toward the building. "Secure the device and get out the back way."

Teller closed the lid, latching the hasps on the case, and Traynor ran across to where Thurston stood. A hailstorm of gunfire erupted from the latest arrivals and bullets peppered the exterior of the building close to the doorway. "Who the hell are these guys?" he growled.

"Do you want me to ask?"

"Maybe next time."

Traynor glanced back and saw Teller making his way back toward the rear of the building. "Time to go, ma'am."

Thurston nodded. "OK."

Outside, the rear of the building was littered with bricks and all kinds of other junk. It explained what had happened to everything that had been inside the building, having been moved and dumped haphazardly out back. It created a bizarre maze for the team to navigate through for their escape route.

"This is shit," Teller said aloud.

"You can say that again," Traynor agreed.

They followed Thurston through the labyrinth of unwanted items. They'd made it about halfway through before the first shooter appeared in the doorway and opened fire. Thurston and the others fell flat as bullets played a strangely melodic racket as they ricocheted from an abundance of metallic objects.

They were soon joined by the rest of their compatriots; the noise gradually crescendoed into an almost deafening roar.

"I guess we're kinda pinned down!" Traynor shouted over the din.

"You think?" Thurston said.

Then suddenly the noise died, and they glanced at each other with wary looks. A voice called out, "Americans? Can you hear me?"

"Little hard not to," Traynor muttered as he rammed a fresh mag home into his M17. He unscrewed his suppressor, wanting to hear the result of doing something to save their asses.

"What do you want?" Thurston called back.

"I think you know the answer to that question."

"I guess I do."

The accent on the man was thick. Thurston turned to Teller. "Any luck with the comms?"

"No, ma'am."

"Keep moving through this damned maze of shit. See if you can find a way out. If they get in behind us, we're screwed."

Teller nodded and did as he was ordered, taking the case with him.

"I am waiting for an answer, American."

"You'll kill us either way, asshole," Thurston shouted back.

"It is just a minor technicality. Now, stop wasting my time. If you are waiting for help from your friends, then you are sadly mistaken."

Using just hand signals the general indicated for Traynor to move back in the direction that Teller took. Keeping low, they started weaving their way through the jumble of junk. They hadn't gone far when the attackers opened up once more.

Bullets tore through the air and hammered into the detritus. Thurston and Traynor caught up to Teller at the edge of the junk field. Straight away, they could see why he had stopped. With the jumble of rubbish having ended, they were now faced with an open area of perhaps thirty meters between them and the next bit of cover which, as luck would have it, was a low fence made out of rocks.

Thurston muttered a curse and thought for a moment. They were literally between a rock and a hard place. She reached into her pocket and dug out her cell. As soon as she looked at the screen, she cursed her stupidity.

She looked at the two men with her. "Well?"

"Seems to me we're fucked either way, ma'am," Teller said.

"I'm with him," Traynor agreed.

Thurston nodded. "Lock and load."

Kandahar, Afghanistan

"How far out are the ATS?" Ferrero asked Swift.

"Couple of minutes."

"Let's hope they can hang on that long."

They both stared at the large screen. Although comms was still down, the computer tech was able to get visual back up. They saw their people move through the rubbish which then opened out onto the expanse beyond it. Then watched as the ensuing discussion decided on their next move. Ferrero frowned. "What are they doing?"

"Not sure."

A few heartbeats later they watched on in horror as their three team members stood up.

"Aw shit no."

Chandigarh, India

The three M17s blasted off rounds like there was no tomorrow. Thurston, Traynor, and Teller just kept squeezing the triggers as fast as they could, at any target which presented itself to them. It was a ploy designed to throw their enemies off-balance. And it worked, for about ten seconds. It was at that point that two 5.56mm rounds punched into Traynor's torso and knocked him off his feet.

"Christ!" Thurston blurted out and fired at the shooter responsible. The man took both rounds in the vest and fell to the ground, stunned. Then the general dropped down beside her fallen man. Teller was already checking him out.

"He's fucked up pretty bad, ma'am. He needs a medivac."

Traynor ground his teeth against the worsening pain. "I'm OK."

"Sure, you are," Teller nodded as he tried to staunch the flow of blood. He looked at Thurston and shook his head.

More anger surged through her, and she rose and rattled off more shots in their attackers' direction before dropping back down.

"Can you stop the blood?" she asked Teller.

"I'm trying, ma'am."

Suddenly they were taking fire from a different direction. The bad guys were trying to flank them.

Thurston scooped up Traynor's fallen M17 and lurched back to her feet. This time both weapons let loose with a furious storm of lead. She felt the burn of a bullet as it sliced through her T-shirt sleeve just above the bicep. The lead cut a shallow furrow through flesh and then passed on.

With a hiss of pain, she took a knee and examined the wound. "You're lucky that wasn't your head, ma'am," Teller pointed out.

"I'm reasonably sure it soon will be, Pete. Especially if we don't get out of here."

"Sirens," Traynor gasped. "I...hear si–sirens."

Thurston and Teller looked at him, thinking that he was hallucinating because of his blood loss. But then the sound filtered through the rattle of gunfire. Traynor had been right; there were sirens.

"He's right," Teller said.

The gunfire died away and stopped, making the sirens more distinct, louder. Thurston risked a look over the top of the detritus and saw that the shooters had disappeared. "They've gone."

"Ma'am, you need to take the suitcase and get out of here. Go to the safehouse."

She shook her head.

"Listen to me, if I take my hands away from these holes there's a good chance Pete will bleed out. Take the device and go," murmured Teller, concentrating his efforts on his wounded teammate.

"Damn it –"

"Get out! We'll be fine. Take our guns."

Thurston nodded and gathered the weapons. She then tucked them inside her pants and picked up the suitcase. "I'll do what I can for you both."

"We won't be hard to find."

Without glancing back, Thurston disappeared over the stone wall on the other side of the open area.

Kandahar, Afghanistan

"Damn it!" Ferrero cursed. "This is all fucked up. Someone get me General Jones."

"I'm here," Jones said as he entered the room. "What's happened, Luis?"

"The second team was hit when they were securing the device."

Concern etched Jones' face. "Who are these people?"

"We're not sure. I do have, however, at least one operator down. Possibly KIA and another with him about to be taken into custody by the ATS. And Mary is out there somewhere carrying a suitcase full of nuclear weapon."

"Who's down?"

"Pete, Traynor."

"Have you talked to them?"

Ferrero shook his head. "Whoever did it, jammed

the signals. And now that the ATS is on-site it's virtually impossible."

"What about Mary?"

"I was about to try her."

"Do it."

"Bravo, copy?"

"Copy, Zero."

Thank God. "Sitrep, Bravo."

"I'm making for the safehouse with the package, over."

"OK, send me your coordinates, and I'll have someone come pick you up."

"We need to see to Traynor and Teller."

"I'll do that," Jones interrupted.

"The general will see to that, Mary."

"OK. I'll wait for a ride then."

"One'll be along shortly."

"I'll send you my numbers."

"OK."

Thurston's position became clear a minute or so later, and help was dispatched. Ferrero walked across to Swift. "Slick, is there anything you can tell me about these people?"

"I've had one hit from facial recognition," the tech told Ferrero.

"Who?"

"He's a Chechen by the name of Khasan Islamov. Wanted by the Russians for a bombing in Rostov. Apparently, he has contacts in the world of all things that go bang. Mainly these two."

Swift went silent, and two pictures came up side-by-side on the screen. "Ibragim Barayev and Madina Umarov. If Islamov is bad, these two are worse. They were behind the bombing of a theatre in Moscow, a hotel in Kyiv Ukraine, another in Volgograd, plus the assassination of more than one Russian minister. Our friend Vlad had sent out more than one kill team over the past few years to find this pair, and none of them have returned."

"Christ," Hank Jones hissed.

"Suffice to say," said Ferrero, "that these two are behind the seizure of the other device."

"It is a reasonably safe bet," Swift agreed.

"Which also means that they're not likely to give up on the suitcase that Mary has."

"Correctamundo."

"Tell the pickup team to move faster, the sooner she's in the safehouse, the better."

"That still leaves Scimitar and his team," Jones pointed out.

"Yes, it does."

CHAPTER ELEVEN

Xinjiang Province, China

Like the others, Jin Zhāng had changed vehicles and he lurched in the seat of the truck as it hit another hole in the gravel road. He turned and stared at the driver while cursing him in Pashto. The Pakistani SSG man apologized and immediately hit another hole.

To their east was a line of snow-capped mountains shrouded by a low mist. The valley which they traveled through was a mix of greens and browns. They still had two more days of driving until they reached Ürümqi where they would leave the vehicle hidden at the Grand Bazaar until time ran out and it detonated.

If he thought he could get it all the way to Bejing, then that's what Zhāng would have preferred, but perhaps it would be best served in Ürümqi.

They continued driving, the state of the road slowly deteriorating the further they went. The driver slowed as he negotiated a deeply rutted bend where the inner curve dropped away into a gully. The road straightened once more along flat ground, then stretched gradually toward a low hill.

The MH-6 suddenly appeared in front of the truck, seeming to rise from the ground. On each of the helicopter's skids were two heavily armed operators. All wore full tactical gear and balaclavas.

The truck lurched to a halt, and Zhāng slapped the dash frantically. "Back up! Back up!"

The gears grated as the driver jammed the stick into reverse. The truck began moving only to be stopped by a second MH-6 with more armed men dropping in behind them.

The men from both helicopters dismounted. Their FN F2000s raised and pointed at the truck. Zhāng paled. What was happening? Who were these people?

Gunfire rattled out from behind the truck as the newcomers killed the SSG men. Beside Zhāng the windscreen was shattered when a round passed through it and punched a hole into the driver's head.

Then they were there. The door was flung open, and the shooter who stood there raised his weapon and shot Zhāng twice with a handgun. He then turned and with a heavily accented voice called out, "Hurry up. We have five minutes before the Chinese response team arrives."

The truck rocked, and a man appeared from behind carrying the device which they sought. "I have it here."

"Good, back onto the helicopters," the leader snapped, a moment before a round from a Chinese QBU-88 sniper rifle punched into the side of his head.

———————

"Now, take out the helicopters," Hunt ordered Mike "Popeye" Oil.

"Copy that," Popeye said calmly as he shifted his aim. "Where did these fuckers come from?"

"Who knows?" Hunt replied as he opened fire with his QBZ-95 Bullpup style Chinese assault rifle. Before the team had deployed, they'd swapped out almost all their equipment for Chinese stuff and jumped clean with no identifying marks or insignia on their uniforms. "Gunner, call this in. Tell them that the op is all fucked up and we're trying to secure the device."

"Roger that."

"Rucker, on me."

Hunt came out of the dead ground and brought the Bullpup up to his shoulder. He could sense rather than see his combat medic's presence. Both men had flicked their weapons onto semi-auto and were starting to pick their targets as they pressed forward. A new gun joined the battle, and he guessed that Jenkins had now joined them. Up ahead the surprised shooters seemed to mill about, their confusion, at having lost their commander, evident on their faces and in their actions.

Hunt dropped a man with a well-placed shot and then switched to another and fired again. The three of them plus Popeye dealt with the shooters quickly and efficiently. So much so that the rotors on the helicopters were still spinning.

"Get the suitcase," Hunt ordered Jenkins.

"Scimitar, copy?" His comms came to life.

"Copy."

"There are four vehicles and a helo headed in your direction. Approximately two mikes out. You need to make yourself small fast."

"Copy that. Out."

Hunt looked about. "No time to hang around. Let's go, in the trees. Popeye watch our sixes."

The firefight had been brief and brutal, and now it was time to leave. They had only just made the trees when the first of the Chinese trucks appeared. Hunt pressed his talk button. "Popeye, you need to act like a worm and move along that dead patch of ground until you can get into the trees at the far end."

"Copy, Boss. I'm moving."

While Popeye moved toward the trees, Hunt watched the trucks pull up. The troops dismounted and set up a shallow perimeter. Then the commanding officer and two others took in the scene of carnage before them.

A sound reached Hunt's ears. It was a low WHOP-WHOP sound, the noise of a fast-approaching helicopter.

"Popeye, you need to shift your ass before that helo gets here or they'll be all over you."

"I'm almost there."

"Move faster."

Suddenly the large machine roared overhead. A Harbin Z-19 attack/reconnaissance helicopter, China's modern version of the Bell AH-1 Cobra. It began swinging lazy circles over the target area looking for anything of interest.

"Popeye, where are you?"

"I made it into the trees. Be with you in a minute."

"Copy that."

As Hunt watched the Chinese, their posture changed, and they began looking in the direction of the trees where he and his team were hiding. Understanding the ramifications of being found there, he turned to Rucker and said, "It's time we left."

Kandahar, Afghanistan

Hank Jones could tell by the look on Ferrero's face

that the news was bad. "Rip the band-aid off, Luis. Don't sugar-coat it."

"Chief Hunt's team has an ongoing problem," Ferrero told him. "The target was attacked by two teams transported by helicopters. Hunt and his team were able to eliminate the threat and secure the package. However, the incursion by the other teams triggered a rapid response from the Chinese; who are now in pursuit of the SEAL team."

"Great day in the fucking morning," Jones muttered. "Where are they at?"

"Their overwatch team is in constant contact with them and are trying to guide them to safety. But, and this is a big but, they still have to make it across the border without being seen."

"And they still have the device?"

"Yes."

"Tell them they need to shake their tail and find a reasonably secure place for an extract."

"You're going to send an air asset to get them out?"

"Damn right, I am. There's no way in hell I'm leaving them out there with their asses in the wind. Especially with a nuclear weapon."

"There is one other problem," Ferrero pointed out.

Jones knew what he meant and nodded. "There is that."

"These terrorists have been one step ahead of us most of the time. It's just sheer luck that we've only lost one of the nukes."

"So far," Jones said.

"The question is, where the hell are they getting their intel from?"

"Sir?" Swift appeared at their sides. "I think I might know where they are."

Lahore, Pakistan

Barayev hung up the encrypted satellite phone and cursed loudly. Madina looked across at him and asked, "What is the problem?"

"We have lost the team in China. Our source said that the team the Americans sent killed them and took the nuclear weapon with them."

Madina nodded. "It is only a minor problem. We still have one."

"I wanted three," he hissed back at her, eyes sparking with fire.

"There is still the second one in India," she pointed out.

He nodded. "Yes. Call Khasan, I know exactly where it will be going."

Kane looked at the others and said, "Change of mission. Slick has a possible location for our friends who stole the device."

"Do we know who they are, yet?" Cara asked.

Both she and Axe had rejoined the team after escaping the ambush, and now they were all in the safehouse run by the NSA.

"Hard-liners led by a dick called Ibragim Barayev and his lovely lady friend, Madina Umarov. They're wanted all over Europe but mainly in Vlad's backyard. They are serious professionals who have co-ordinated other attacks on Thurston's team in India and Hunt in China."

"What's the news on the others?" Axe asked as he dabbed at the cut on his forearm.

Kane's face was grim. "Thurston got away with the device."

"And?" Brick prompted.

"Traynor took a round and is in bad shape. Teller stayed with him to try and keep him alive. The Indian ATS were on site when anything was last heard."

A dark silence overcame the group, and it was a short while before Arenas asked, "What about the SEALs?"

"They secured their package but are now being chased all over China by the PLA."

"This is fucked," Axe growled.

"Amen to that, Brother," Brick agreed.

"Where can we find these assholes, Reaper?" Cara asked, a hard edge to her voice.

"An apartment block in the north of Lahore. Apparently Slick tracked them there. Only problem is, that part of Lahore is run by the Pakistani Mafia."

Axe raised his eyebrows. "Is there such a thing?"

"There is," said a tall man standing in the corner.

"Great. Why is it that whenever we go to a country, they organize to have their resident bad guys fuck up our day?"

The man who had spoken was an NSA operative who went by the name of Mr. White. It was obviously not the name he was born with, but it's what they called him. Kane assumed he had some kind of 'spook' complex. He said, "These people are not to be messed with if you can help it. They deal in arms, assassination, drugs, even landgrabs, believe it or not. They also have tentacles in the Pakistan government."

"We don't plan on messing with them," Kane said. "Just going to see if our bad guys are in the neighborhood."

"If they are, you can bet the Mafia know about them too. More than likely they've paid for the privilege of being there."

"You mean protection?" Kane asked.

"Uh-huh."

"Why would they do that if they know that these Chechens have a nuclear weapon?"

"Unless they don't," Mr. White said.

"Unless they don't," Kane agreed, a thought germinating in his brain. "And that is our way in."

"What do you mean?" Axe asked.

"We're going to have a chat with the man in charge."

The big ex-recon marine shook his head. "This is going to be a bad fucking idea."

———————

Chandigarh, India

There were three NSA agents in the safehouse with Thurston. All were armed and expecting trouble, especially after Ferrero reached out about the China incident. Their commander was an agent named Dick Rose, a native of Baltimore.

"General," he said, "I was just talking to the CIA, and they will have a team here within two hours to take the package off our hands."

Thurston nodded as she stared out the window at the distant sunset of pink and red. "Is there any news of my men?"

"You've not talked to the general?"

She turned. "No."

"From what we can gather, your man in the hospital is in surgery, and the other is being interrogated by the ATS."

"Shit, we have to get him out."

"Not much we can do at the moment. We're in

lockdown until the device is gone."

"Damn it!"

Thurston turned back to the window. Outside, the lawn was almost perfectly manicured, the gardens clipped and tidy. It was something you would expect to see in one of India's royal palaces rather than an NSA safehouse. Which she guessed was why it remained so secure. "Is there any news about the people who attacked us?"

"No. Not a word, other than what your people have already disclosed."

"They won't give up."

"Maybe not."

Thurston reached down and took her M17 out of its holster. She checked it for about the hundredth time and then put it back. Rose said, "Do you want something more than that?"

The general looked at him questioningly. "Like what?"

"Come into the library, as the British call it."

She followed him out of the living room and into the library. The NSA man walked over to a wood panel in the wall and touched it. the panel clicked back, and Rose pulled it open to reveal a small myriad of weapons. He reached for an MP5, but Thurston stopped him. "I'll take the CQBR if it's all the same to you?"

Rose shrugged and selected it from the rack. Then he took out some spare magazines and boxes of ammunition. "You'll have to load them yourself."

Thurston understood why. Loaded magazines left sitting around unused for great lengths of time sometimes caused creasing. She opened a box and started to load one of the magazines. Rose watched her with fascination. "You never seen a woman do something like this before?"

"Not with the ease you do it."

"Practice, I guess."

Once she had three, Thurston slapped one of them home and jacked a 5.56 round into the breech.

Another agent poked his head in through the door. "We've got movement out the west side."

Rose nodded. "Let's go take a look."

They hurried through the house, Rose taking the MP5 with him. He and Thurston took up positions either side of a large window and stared out. The glare of the setting sun filled the room, making it difficult to see. The general squinted against the harsh rays as she tried to see outside.

"You see anything?" she asked Rose.

"Not a thing. This sun is a bitch."

"Look out!"

The cry of alarm came from Thurston as she dropped to the carpeted floor. It was followed by an explosion which rocked the building. Dust and debris rained down on top of her, ears ringing, and she was unable to hear much at all. The general raised her head and blinked to clear her eyes.

Through the dust fog, she could see Rose lying on the floor, mouth open screaming as he clutched at his leg which had been impaled by a large wood splinter. The problem was, she couldn't really hear his screams because of the blast.

Thurston turned her head to the right and saw that where the window had once been, a large, jagged hole was now visible. She staggered to her feet, glass, dirt, and debris falling away from her clothing. She could taste the dust in the air with each breath she took.

A frown creased Thurston's brow as she saw tiny explosions all around her. In her confused state, it took longer than was prudent to work out what was happening. She was being shot at.

With a shout of rage, Thurston brought up the CQBR and squeezed the trigger. A figure filled the opening. Shrouded in dust-filled sunlight. Whoever it was, jerked violently under the impact of the bullet strikes.

The gunfire sounded distant, but Thurston's hearing was starting to return. She raised the weapon to her shoulder and looked for another target. Two more figures filled the void, automatic weapons in their grip.

Thurston fired, and the two intruders ducked for cover. The general sidestepped across to where Rose lay. She reached down and grasped his collar. "Hold on."

The muscles in her shoulder bunched as she took

the strain and then began dragging the wounded man across the floor.

One of the shooters appeared in the hole, and Thurston caught sight of him before he could fire. She pointed the CQBR in the general direction and squeezed the trigger. The weapon bucked in her hand and stitched a line of bullets from one side of the opening to the other, catching the intruder in the process.

The killer fell back out of view, and Thurston managed to get Rose through the doorway before another object flew into the already devastated room. The general glanced at it and saw the cylindrical shape of an M84 Flashbang sitting on the floor.

Thurston ducked in behind the wall, shut her eyes tight, and opened her mouth to lessen the effects of the coming blast. Still, it wasn't much, and it rang her bell reasonably well.

She had to shake it off quickly because she knew they would be coming. Somewhere in the house, more gunfire rang out, which immediately indicated that the others were engaged as well. It was also a good sign because it meant her hearing was returning even after the flashbang had detonated.

Thurston glanced around the corner of the doorway and saw three men entering the room through the gaping hole. She squeezed off two shots and heard one of the men cry out before he fell to the floor. She was certain that it wasn't a mortal shot because she'd hit him square in the body armor he was wearing.

The response from the intruders was a crazy fusillade of shots that tore holes through the plaster wall and punched into the one on the far side. Fine dust and chunks of debris rained down all around Thurston and Rose. She ground her teeth together and muttered a curse. "Fucking assholes."

Thurston leaned around the corner and unloaded the rest of her clip. Beside her, Rose tried to drag himself along the short hallway out of danger. He was getting nowhere fast, and instead, he shouted at Thurston in a hoarse voice, "The library! Get to the library! You'll find everything you need."

Slapping home a fresh magazine, Thurston shook her head. "I'm not leaving you."

"Somethings are more important. Give me your weapon."

"Damn it, Rose," she cursed.

"Do it and get out of here to the library. Like I said, you'll find what you need."

Thurston came to her feet and hurried to the library. Behind her, she heard the CQBR fire a couple of short bursts. In the library, she opened the hidden cupboard and let her gaze roam over the weapons.

M249 SAW.

The general grasped it and then looked for some box magazines which went with it. She then found a couple of belts and a vest. A couple of minutes later, Thurston was ready to return to the fray. And she was good and mad and loaded for bear.

She found the other two NSA agents at the front of the house. One was wounded but still in the fight, while the other seemed to be fine. They were pinned down behind a low internal wall which was becoming gradually more shredded with the continuing volume of fire the attackers were pouring through it.

Thurston opened fire with the SAW, its chatter filling the house. Holes appeared in walls as she moved the weapon from right to left cutting across and hitting one of the shooters with at least three rounds. She saw an eruption of blood spurting from the wounds, and he screamed with pain. Not wanting to stop, she used all the firepower at her disposal and burned through what remained of the two-hundred round magazine with devastating effect.

Everything stopped. The gunfire ceased in what became a stunned silence. Thurston dropped the SAW and took out her M17. "Watch our six," she ordered the uninjured agent as she walked forward.

The handgun was held at eye height as she scanned the area before her. There were four of them, all but one was dead. The general turned and walked back toward where she'd left Rose, discovering him lying open-eyed in the short hallway, dead.

A tentative look around the shattered doorway into the room told her it was clear. The attackers had gone. Maybe the sound of the SAW scared them off. Whatever it was, it didn't matter. What did matter was that the device was still secure.

CHAPTER TWELVE

Lahore, Pakistan

"I still think this is a bad idea," Axe said. "Good way to get killed if you ask me. Ever see that trick in the circus when the lion tamer sticks his head in the lion's mouth?"

"What about it?" asked Kane.

"That's us. Only it's our dicks going in, and the lion is about to chow down on them."

"I hope he's not looking to get a feed out of yours," Kane said with a wry smile.

"Very funny."

Kane said, "You still with us back there?"

"Roger that," Cara said though his earpiece.

"Good. Once we get there, you three sit about a block back and try to stay out of trouble."

"I could say the same to you," Cara shot back. "About the trouble, I mean."

They were headed for a restaurant called Gulshan Grill, named after the owner, Gulshan Anand. It was where Aziz Zoman, the head of the Pakistani Mafia ate regularly, and word had it that he would be there that evening. Most likely with enough bodyguards to start a small war.

"We're almost there," Mr. White said from behind the wheel of the SUV.

"OK, Cara, drop back."

"Copy."

Kane and Axe checked the loads in their M17s and then tucked them in behind their backs in the waistband of their pants. Mr. White said, "Tell me if you don't want me to stop, I'll just keep driving."

Lights flashed past as did the Lahore night. Neon signs illuminated many of the businesses. It was like a satellite city in the northern part of Lahore itself; however, most of it belonged to one man.

"Does this guy have a thing for the Vegas strip or what?" Axe commented.

"All it took was one visit," Mr. White agreed. "And then he was hooked."

"So, he built all this on his criminal empire?" Kane asked.

"That's about it. Here we are."

The SUV pulled over to the curb and all within looked to their right at the restaurant. Like everything else, it had a flashing neon sign out front. On both sides of the entrance doors stood a Pakistani dressed in a black suit. Slung over their shoulders were Russian-made PP-2000s. Kane said, "Cara, there are two shooters on the front door."

"Copy, Reaper."

"Leave the weapons, Axe" Kane ordered retrieving his M17 and putting it in the glove compartment.

"Just what I like to do," he growled, passing the M17 to Kane. "Going into a den of rattlers without a stick to kill them with."

The three of them climbed from the vehicle and approached the door. The two guards eyed them cautiously and then stepped casually in front of them, preventing further passage for the trio. Guard number one, a thickset man with a thin mustache, said in heavily accented English, "Go home."

"We're looking to get something to eat," Kane said. "Home is a long way away."

"Find somewhere else to eat," the man said as he dropped his hand to the PP-2000 in a threatening gesture.

"That's not neighborly of you, friend. All we want is to get us something to eat, and you just had to touch your gun."

"Fu—"

Kane's right fist shot out and struck the man in the throat. The guard dropped to his knees, gasping for breath. Kane then brought his knee up, and it hit the guard flush in the face knocking him out before he even touched the pavement.

Meanwhile, Axe had taken down the second guard with a flurry of blows after he froze while watching what happened to his friend.

The three men pushed in through the door, and Mr. White said, "You two really know how to make friends."

"We're right nice when you get to know us," Axe said with a grin.

"Uh, huh."

Inside the restaurant, it looked more like a casino than a place to eat. In fact, the whole grill thing was just a front for illegal gambling. And of course, with the wealth which graced the tables within, came the armed guards. Behind Kane, Axe said, "I told you this was a fucking bad idea."

A young Pakistani woman walked up to them, a folder in her hand. She was dressed head to toe in a red dress, the shiny fabric covering every inch of the woman's skin, apart from her hands and face, which was the only flesh left exposed. "Can I help you, gentlemen?"

"We're here to see Mister Zoman," Kane said.

Her pleasant smile disappeared. "I think you'd better leave."

Kane shook his head. "What is your name?"

"Hira."

Kane nodded. "Well, Hira, we'd like to talk to Mister Zoman. It's a matter of life and death."

"Yours if you don't leave," she said with urgency.

Mister Zoman will kill you for interrupting and me for allowing it."

"What is happening, Hira?" a voice from behind the woman asked.

She closed her eyes in resignation before turning to face the man who had spoken.

"You have to be shitting me," Axe mumbled.

Standing before them, flanked by two large and armed bodyguards, was a solid looking man dressed in white who appeared to have a penchant for Elvis impersonations. Hira turned to face him and said, "Sorry, Mister Zoman. I was just telling these men that they had to leave. However, they were most insistent that they see you."

The Mafia boss took his sunglasses off and stared at the three men. "How did you get in here?"

"Front door is generally a good way," Axe said.

"My men let you in?"

"Not exactly," Kane told him with a shrug of his shoulders.

The Mafia man's eyes narrowed. "We are done here."

His two bodyguards' hands made a move toward their guns. "You touch those things, and I'll make you eat them, motherfuckers," Axe hissed in a low voice.

They hesitated, and Kane took the opportunity to say, "We want two minutes of your time then we'll be gone. I guarantee that what we have to say will make it worth your while."

"You intend to give me money?"

"No, asshole, it might just save your life," Axe growled.

Zoman glared at him. "I do not like you."

"I think I might cry."

"Hira, wait in my office while I talk to these... gentlemen."

"But, Mister Zoman. I tried to get them to leave."

Kane glanced at Mr. White as one of the Mafia man's bodyguards grasped her roughly by the arm and escorted her away. "Come with me," he growled.

They followed him to a table at the rear and sat down. He ordered a drink and asked them, "Would you like one, too?'

"No thanks," said Kane with a shake of his head.

"Well then, tell me what is so important that you would risk death to disturb me?"

What a ⸱ick. Kane said, "We believe you are giving shelter to some Chechens."

Zoman just stared at him, but Kane could tell there was something to his words because the Mafia man changed the set of his jaw. "What makes you think that?"

"Just call it a hunch," Kane answered. "I don't really care that you're giving them refuge, but they have something that we need to get back."

"I don't know anything about any Chechens."

"Don't make me call you a liar," Kane warned

him. "It kind of gets upsetting when you do that. Especially when that something I'm after happens to be a suitcase nuke."

That got his attention.

"You didn't know that, huh?" Kane allowed. He glanced at Mr. White. "He didn't know that."

"I guess he didn't."

"What are you talking about?" Zoman demanded.

Kane's voice grew hard. "I'm talking about Bara-yev and Umarov, and the fact that they have a nu-clear device in your neighborhood. That's what I'm talking about."

"You lie!"

"Why the hell would I lie? We've been chasing down three devices – three! The one that went off in Kashmir was part of a bigger scheme. These terror-ists killed or tried to kill all those transporting them. Now they have one of them right here under your nose, asshole. Are you going to help us or not?"

"I will take you there."

"No, just tell Mister White how to get there, and we'll take care of it."

"OK."

"Now, I want the girl you just took to your office."

"No."

"Axe, go get her."

"On it, Reaper."

"I said no!" Zoman snarled and reached for a SIG P226 beneath the left side of his white coat.

Kane's hands blurred in a flurry of movement, and before the Mafia man knew it, he was staring down the barrel of his own handgun. "We don't have time for this, shit."

Zoman nodded, and Kane said, "Now, speak."

A minute later, Zoman had told Mr. White all he needed to know. Two minutes after that, Axe returned with the young lady in tow, a small cut on his bottom lip. "What happened to you?" Kane asked him.

"Forgot to duck," he said with a wry smile. He stared at the Mafia man. "Your boy is having a little sleep about now, but he'll be fine."

"What are you doing?" Hira asked.

Kane said, "You can come with us, or you can stay here. Your choice."

Even though Hira knew what could happen to her if she stayed, she hesitated. Her nervous gaze darted to her boss. "Hey," Kane snapped. "Look at me, not him. You come with us right now, and you'll be safe."

Zoman could have let it happen. Bided his time and then fixed the problem after the Americans had gone. But, no. The thought of him losing face in his own illegal casino, in front of all these people did not sit well with him. "If you go, I will have you killed and your family, too."

Kane shook his head, and Axe glanced at Mr. White. He said, "Didn't I tell you this was a fucking bad idea?"

"I sure wish you hadn't said that Mister Zoman," was all Kane said before he shot him.

The Mafia man dropped like a stone, clutching at his knee. The howls of pain started not long afterward. The Team Reaper leader stepped forward and grabbed a handful of oily hair. He tilted the man's head back and looked at the anguished face. "Be thankful I never put it into your head. However, I will come back to kill you if something happens to the young lady. So, you see, it's in your best interest to keep her out of harm's way. Understand?"

Zoman nodded.

"What's wrong? You look a little all shook up."

"You did not just do that?" Axe growled incredulously.

"Do what?"

"You know, Teddy Bear."

"I'm not the only one, Hound Dog."

"Are you lonesome tonight?"

"Are you two quite done?" Cara's voice interrupted over the comms.

Axe smiled at Kane. "Your mama don't like me."

Kane raised his eyebrows.

"Oh, come on, Reaper. Suzie Q? You don't know her?"

"You forty-eight crashed, buddy, let's go."

"I knew you knew her," Axe said gleefully and followed his friend toward the door. Then he called out, "Hey, Reaper, you know we already knew where the bad guys were right?"

"What's your point?" Kane called back over his shoulder.

———————

Three blocks were all they had to travel to reach their destination. Thanks to the NSA, the team were armed with CQBRs and wore tactical vests. Kane said, "Two stairwells, two teams. I'll take Axe and Mister White, Cara with Brick and Carlos."

Arenas asked, "Can I take point on this one?"

Cara nodded. "Sure, why?"

"I'm a happily married man, Señora," Arenas told her. "And for me to follow you up the stairs with your ass in my face might lead to impure thoughts."

Axe laughed out loud as Cara shook her head. "You're a dick."

Kane said, "He is right though you do have a nice ass."

"Enough about my ass already. Let's go get some bad guys."

That was all it took to break the tension of the upcoming mission. Now they switched back on and moved with precision towards the apartment block.

"Remember, Reaper Two, third floor, third door."

"Sounds like poetry, Reaper."

"Just as long as it's not a eulogy."

Taking the stairs two at a time at a brisk clip,

they soon arrived at the landing, beginning to make their way along it until Kane stopped suddenly with a muttered a curse. There was a third stairwell which he assumed led to the back. "Axe, keep an eye out here."

"Copy that."

With Axe on the landing at the top of the stairs, Kane and Mr. White moved on until they stopped outside the door they wanted, opposite Arenas. Nodding to each other, they stepped back and breached.

Arenas went in first. Beyond the door was a short hallway which would have acted as a funnel had there been someone expecting them. He moved out into the living room and swept left, while Cara, who was hot behind him, swept right and into the kitchen.

Kane and Brick broke off and swept two bedrooms while Mr. White swept the third. Cries of 'Clear!' erupted through the apartment as each team member finished. They all congregated in the living area, and Kane said, "We're too late."

"They can't have been gone long," Cara explained. "There's still a hot pot on the stove in the kitchen."

"Check everything, see if they've left anything that'll help us out."

"You figure our friend Zoman warned them?" Mr. White asked Kane.

"You figured that too, huh?"

"Something like that."

"Maybe I should have shot him in the head after all."

"Maybe."

Kane thought about Hira for a moment and knew she was going to be in trouble. He should never have let her go after they left the illegal casino.

"Zero? Reaper One, over."

"Read you, Reaper One."

"No joy on the package or the HVTs. We'll sweep the apartment and disappear."

"Roger that, I'll have Swift sift through everything he can find, and we'll see what he can come up with. Anything else?"

"The girl that got caught up with our operation."

"What about her?"

"I have a feeling that she may be in trouble."

"We don't have time for this, Reaper."

"Yes, I know."

"OK, I'll see what I can come up with."

"Thanks, Luis."

"Zero out."

Axe hurried in through the open apartment door. "Reaper, we got problems."

"What now?"

"There's three SUVs inbound along the street. They don't look like something that your average Joe would own."

Kane hurried outside and looked from the landing down onto the street. The vehicles were almost at a stop. They were white, and the lead one's plate read 'King'.

"Everybody finish up what you're doing. Elvis just arrived with his roadies."

"You want to fight or run?" Axe asked.

Before he could answer, he was joined by the others. Cara saw the doors open, and a dozen armed men climb out, Zoman being one of the first, a bandage around his leg and a good limp. "He's a tough one, Reaper," Axe growled as they watched him direct his men.

"Mister White, does this guy run drugs?"

"Amongst other things."

"OK then, let's put him out of business."

They opened fire as the mafia men raced toward the building. It was a massacre. Trained professionals against would-be killers. Six went down in the first volley, Zoman included. After that, the fight went out of the remainder, and they ran away. Sometimes the fight went that way.

"Let's go," Kane ordered.

New Delhi, India

The CIA put on a helicopter which took both Thurston and the device to the Embassy in New Delhi. On her arrival, it was dark out, and feeling exhausted, she was ushered inside while the rotors were still spinning on her ride, and taken to see Paul Adams, the Ambassador.

Adams was a gray-haired man with deep lines across his face from either age or worry, no one could tell which, but probably the latter. India was his most recent posting and had been for the past couple of years, after having been transferred from Pakistan. And before that, Egypt.

The ambassador stared at her for a moment before saying, "You've had it rough."

"Yes, sir."

"I've been told to help you any way I can, General."

"The device, sir?"

"It will be sent Stateside in the next day or so."

"My men, who are in Chandigarh?"

"The wounded man is still in surgery and the other – we aren't sure."

"I was told that the ATS had him."

Adams nodded. "The last we heard that was right. They've shifted him though, and we don't know where."

"Damn it. You know what they'll do to him, don't you?"

Again, a nod. "I have an idea."

"Let me tell you just to refresh your memory. They'll torture him to get every bit of information out of him that he knows. Hell, even stuff that he doesn't. Teller is a good man, but he can't hold out against them forever. And when he does crack, they'll learn about the nuclear devices, and they'll go after Pakistan even harder. The whole region will go up in flames."

"We're almost there as it is," Adams pointed out.

"Which is why I need to get back there. Teller needs to be gotten out of wherever he is being held before they can torture it out of him. They'll already know about the Chechen link if their intelligence people are any good."

"Do you need any help?" Adams asked.

"What have you got?"

"What do you need?"

"Military Intelligence?"

"Yes."

"Delta?"

Adams nodded. "One or two."

"Can I borrow your phone?"

"Sure."

"Thanks. I'm not sure how it's going to go."

He left her to the room and went outside to the outer office and closed the door behind him. Thurston picked up the handpiece and punched in a number.

"Jones."

"Sir, it's Mary."

"Good to hear your voice, Mary. Are you OK?"

She sighed, suddenly feeling weary. "I've been better, sir."

"I bet you have. What can I do for you?"

She told him about the situation with Teller and

waited for his response. "You want to bust him out?" Jones asked.

"Yes, sir."

"All right. You'll have to go in dark. If you're caught, you know what that means?"

"Yes, sir. There are some people here at the embassy who can be utilized for the operation. I'm a little worried about Pete Traynor, though."

"Don't worry about him. I'll take care of it. I'm already working on it. However, they wouldn't budge on Teller which is why I'm green-lighting this op. Once Traynor is stable enough, he'll be flown to Ramstein."

"Thank you, General."

"Just don't get caught, Mary. If you do, you're on your own."

CHAPTER THIRTEEN

Xinjiang Autonomous Region, China

They'd been on the run for two days, and now, with the sun about to reach its zenith, the team were about done in. Hunt stopped them just below the crest of a low brush-covered ridge. In the distance to their west were high snow-capped mountains. Beyond those was the border into Afghanistan. Perhaps another two days of hard marching.

So far, they'd been able to keep the pursuing Chinese at arm's length, but Hunt figured it was only a matter of when, not if, they caught up with them. "Take five," Hunt panted. "Gunner, you're on security."

"Copy that."

"How much longer you figure, Chief?" Rucker asked.

"Couple of days."

"These bastards don't give up easy."

"That they don't. How you doing, Popeye?"

"I'm fine, Chief."

Hunt's eyes suddenly took on a thousand-yard stare. The other two SEALs watched him with anticipation. They'd seen it before. "Get under cover!" he snapped. Then into his comms, "Gunner, incoming. Make yourself invisible."

The team scrambled under the brush and waited in silence as though the approaching aircraft might hear them. The beat of the rotors grew steadily louder, and then the Harbin Z-19 attack/reconnaissance helicopter swept over the ridge.

Hunt waited until the sound had dissipated before he reemerged. "Gunner, you got anything back there?"

"Give me a minute, Chief."

"Roger. Popeye, go have a look and see what's on the other side of this damned ridgeline."

"On my way."

Gunner Jenkins appeared through the brush and said, "They're still back there, Chief. Maybe about two miles out."

"All right, on me."

They climbed the rest of the way up the ridge to where Popeye waited for them. The other side was almost a mirror image of the terrain they had already traversed. Hunt studied it for a moment before he said, "These guys behind us figure we're going to head straight for the border. I say we cut to the southwest below this ridgeline and then move north again toward the border. It may put an extra day on our ETA, but if it works, we'll be shuck of the PLA."

"What are we standing around for then?" Rucker asked.

"You two feel that way?" Hunt asked Popeye and Jenkins.

They nodded.

"OK, let's go. Popeye, you're on point."

Kandahar, Afghanistan

Kane and the rest of the team had been back in Afghanistan for twenty-four hours, most of it being downtime to enable them to rest up while Ferrero planned their next move. Axe was making the most of it, laying back in a rubber wading pool with a beer in his hand, no shirt, and sunglasses to protect his eyes from the searing effects of the sun.

Kane, Brick, and Arenas sat at a table under a shade umbrella with more holes in it than a compound out in Helmand Province, playing poker for IOUs. Cara lay back on a battered sun lounge, wearing shorts and a bikini top, reading a copy of Damien Lewis' latest factual account of the SAS titled SAS Italian Job.

"You'll both get sun cancers laying out there like

that," Kane warned them.

"Well come and rub some sunscreen on me then," Cara replied. Then holding her book up, she said, "You should read this book Reaper. These SAS guys back in the second world war were some ballsy people."

"Give it to me when you're finished," Kane told her. He let his eyes linger as he contemplated taking her up on the offer of the sunscreen.

"How many cards you want, Reaper?" Brick asked him, seeing his distracted gaze.

He turned to look at the big ex-SEAL. "Huh?"

"Cards? How many?"

"Oh, three."

Brick gave him the three cards, and Kane drew a third six to go with the two others. Shame it didn't beat Arenas' full house.

Axe lobbed his empty can into an empty forty-four-gallon drum they were using for garbage. "Reaper, throw me another beer."

"I'll have one too," Cara said.

He leaned over to the icebox beside him and retrieved the requested cans, then tossed them to Axe and Cara before looking at the other two. "You want beers as well?"

"Sure."

"Why not?"

"I'll have one," said another voice.

They looked around and saw Reynolds walking

toward them. Kane tossed her a beer and said, "I thought you were working?"

"Downtime. Just like you guys. Slick is still trying to find the Chechens, and Ferrero is watching over the pair looking after Hunt and the SEALs."

"How are they faring?"

Reynolds took off her shirt and exposed a black lacy bra holding a couple of nicely rounded breasts. She saw them looking at her and said, "What? I didn't pack my bikini as Cara did."

She let her hair down and sat next to Kane. "The SEALs are about a day from the border. They managed to lose the PLA unit, which was chasing them, and they still have the nuke."

"Any word on Traynor?"

"Nothing new. General Jones is still working on it."

"What about Teller?"

"Still MIA. You think General Thurston will find him?"

"Between her and Slick I'd say so."

"I hope so. I miss Pete."

"What about me?" Axe called from the pool. "Do you miss me when I'm downrange?"

"Like a hole in the head, Baby."

Things went quiet after that as everyone sipped their beers and thought about their missing team members. The sun still beat down with its burning rays. Axe eventually got sick of the pool and went to join Cara. He pulled the second sun lounge up beside her and asked, "What's the book about?"

"A SAS raid on a German headquarters in World War Two Italy."

"You got another book?"

Cara dropped the book across her chest and gave Axe a quizzical look. "You read?"

"Sure. All the time."

"So how come I've never seen you with a book?"

"Because when we're usually together, we're working," he explained. "You know? Bang! Bang! Bad guys dead."

"All right, I get it. So, you want a book?"

"Yes, what have you got?"

"Fact or fiction?"

"Fact."

"Wait here."

Cara climbed to her feet and walked off to search her bags for the second book she'd brought with her. He noticed the others staring at him. "What?"

Kane said, "You don't read books. The only thing with pages that you read are the latest editions of Playboy. And that's only to look at the pictures."

Axe gave them a wide shit-eating grin. "I'm learning. Broadening my horizons."

They shook their heads and went back to what they were doing. Cara returned with another Damien Lewis book. This one called SAS Ghost Patrol. She handed it over and said, "There. I'll have it back when you're done. I've not read it yet."

"Yes, ma'am," he told her and lay back and started to read.

The crunch of a boot on dry gravel drew the team's attention. "Living it up, I see," Ferrero said with a tired smile.

"Just waiting for the word," Kane replied.

The ex-DEA agent nodded his understanding. "There's a few things happening as we speak. You all know Mary is trying to find Teller. Well, we may have found him. I'm just waiting to hear back from the CIA."

"How's the war shaping up?" Axe asked.

"The US and the European Union are trying to broker a cease-fire."

"That's good news," stated Cara.

"It is. The last thing we need is both India and Pakistan pressing the "Button". The next bit of news isn't so good. You'll be jumping into Chechnya to-morrow night."

"That mean you've got a lead on the suitcase nuke?" Kane inquired.

"No."

"So why are we going to Chechnya?" Brick asked Ferrero.

"Usman Melikov," came the reply. "Actually, it is former General Usman Melikov."

Axe frowned. "Who is he when he's at home?"

"Melikov was one of the commanding generals during the Second Chechen War back in ninety-nine to two thousand. After that, he commanded a group of insurgents. He disappeared for a while, but we think that we may have found him."

"How?" asked Kane.

"Money trail. Don't ask me how Slick does it, but he does. He's in Grozny. You get dropped in, get eyes on. If it is him, then you extract him. Once this gets put into motion, there is only a small window to get you out of there. Most of the city has been rebuilt after the two wars, but there are some areas which are still derelict. We think he is living underground in one such area."

"Why would he do that?" asked Cara. "Obviously he's got money."

"He's in the top five of Russia's most-wanted list," Ferrero explained. "If he sticks his head above ground, they'll cut it off."

"Then why not just tell the Russians?"

"Because we think he's the one behind the Chechen teams. The money anyway. So, if we get him, then we might have an idea what they're up to."

"Even money it's Russia," Axe said.

"Why did you say that?" Cara asked.

"Most likely Siberia."

"Shut up, Axe. Can I shoot him, Luis?"

"Maybe we should leave that to Mary."

A thoughtful smile crossed Cara's face as she stared at Axe. "What is it between you and her, anyway, Stud?"

"She doesn't like me. Simple as that. I've tried to be nice to her, but I don't think she understands me."

"You're scared of her."

"Like you wouldn't believe."

They all chuckled, and Ferrero said, "Briefing will be at fourteen hundred tomorrow, and you'll be wheels up at twenty-hundred. Enjoy the rest of your day and be squared away by tomorrow."

The operations commander turned to walk away. Kane came out of his seat and followed him. "Luis, got a moment?"

"Sure. What is it?"

"These attacks weren't just random, were they?"

"How do you mean?"

"If this Melikov is behind all of this then he needed to be getting intel from somewhere. He's known most of our moves from the start. Someone has been feeding him information from the inside."

"Yes, there's a leak in the NSA, but they're working at plugging it."

"Shit, do they know who?"

"I think so, but they're being non-committal about it all. Miller has one of his men taking care of it."

A concerned expression crossed Kane's face. "Do they know we're going into Chechnya?"

"No, Admiral Joseph and I decided we'd do this one off the books."

"The Admiral is still here?"

"You don't think he'd leave me alone with one of his teams hip-deep in shit, do you? It's OK, it allows me more time to keep an eye on Mary."

"How's she doing?"

"You ought to know the general by now, Reaper. She's pissed and looking for someone to take it out on. I'd hate to be them ATS guys at this time. Especially once she gets her hands on them."

"They won't give Teller over without a fight," Kane said stating the obvious.

"That's why she's taking backup."

"If she gets caught –"

"It'll just be one big shit storm. Seems to be a lot of it going around lately."

"So much for being called the Worldwide Drug Initiative. Might as well just call us One Eight Hundred We Do Everything."

"We do what we're told." The side of Ferrero's mouth lifted in a half-grin.

"Yeah."

"Rest up, Reaper. I have a feeling that Chechnya won't be an easy mission."

National Security Agency, Fort Meade, Maryland

Scott Bald got into work early and was in Kent Miller's office before six. He was nervous, and Miller sensed it. "Did you read the folder?"

"Yes, sir."

"And?"

"And I did some research, and yes, you could be right."

Miller raised his eyebrows. "Could be right? We need to be more certain than that, Scott. Christ, we're about to put a bullet in his fucking head."

"Everything leads back to him, sir. Emails, money trail."

"But something is bothering you? Is that it?"

Bald nodded. "It's sloppy. The trail leads right to this guy's door. What was the one thing a good agent does at all times?"

"Leaves no trail."

"Exactly."

"Maybe this guy is a screwup."

"Maybe."

"You want more time to look into it?"

"Yes, sir."

"I'll give you twenty-four hours."

"Can we bring him in?"

"Why?"

Just in case I'm wrong."

Miller nodded. "As soon as his ass touches his seat, put him in a room."

"Yes, sir."

———————

Two hours later when NSA agent Brett Thomas got off the elevator, he was met by Scott Bald and two other security officers. Alarm filled his eyes when they blocked further passage, and he asked nervously, "What is this?"

"Get back on the elevator, Brett."

His confusion was evident. "What? Why?"

"Just do it. Don't make a scene here."

"Can I at least know why?"

"I'll tell you when we get there."

"Get where?"

"Interrogation."

"Why? What have I done? Damn it, tell me why?" His voice rose for the last word of his sentence.

They ushered him back into the elevator, and the door closed behind them.

When the doors opened again, a solid concrete wall greeted them, its only blemish a sign which read: **Interrogation**, and an arrow that pointed to the left.

The four men walked in the direction the arrow indicated, each aware of the bland, almost sterile hallway. Their footsteps echoed loudly as the heel strikes of their leather shoes pounded the hard floor. They passed numbered doors until they reached the one with the numeral five on it. Bald opened the door and said, "Go in there and sit down."

Thomas did as he was ordered and Bald closed the door behind him. Moving along to the next door in the hallway, Bald opened it and entered the room. Inside he found three other men sitting at electronic equipment used for monitoring interviews. Bald looked through the two-way mirror and saw the door of the interrogation room open. A man in a black suit entered carrying a silver briefcase.

Bald watched on until the man was finished and then asked out loud, "How are we looking?"

"Everything is good," the man closest to him replied.

Bald put in his earpiece. "Let's get started."

When Bald entered the interrogation room, Thomas looked at him and growled with frustration, "What am I doing here?"

"I'll ask the questions," Bald snapped curtly and sat down.

"Fuck you!" Thomas snarled more out of frustration than hostility.

Bald looked down at the manila folder on the table and opened it. He took out two sheets of paper, each with printed emails on them, and pushed them in front of the man opposite. "Read."

"What?"

"Read."

Thomas' blue eyes flickered across the first piece of paper his face passive, but then it changed to one full of confusion. He looked up and opened his mouth to speak, but Bald cut him off. "The next one."

Again, Thomas read this time the second piece

of paper. While he did so, Bald took out the bank statement, then closed the folder.

"These aren't my emails," Thomas said adamantly as he placed the second sheet on the table. "I've never written anything like this."

"Is that your email address at the top?"

Thomas looked at the second one again. "Yes, but I didn't write it."

Bald nodded. "The other piece of paper. The pertinent points have been highlighted."

The NSA man picked it up, and his interrogator said, "You'll note the three payments of one-hundred thousand dollars over the past week."

"The fuck," Thomas blurted out. "There's some mistake. I've never had this much money in my life. Where did it come from?"

"Why don't you tell me?"

"How should I know?"

"It's in your bank account."

"It doesn't mean that I know where it came from."

"Looks bad for you, Brett."

Thomas eyed him cautiously. "What else have you got?"

Bald stared at him for a long moment before he opened the folder again and took out three pictures and laid them in front of Thomas. As he did so, he said their names. "Usman Melikov, Ibragim Barayev, Madina Umarov. All Chechen, and all on the world radar of most wanted assholes."

Confusion returned to Thomas' face. "What do they have to do with this?"

"Melikov was the one who put the money into your bank account. As you know, the other two are involved in the theft of a suitcase nuclear device which we have no idea of the whereabouts. Now the only way he could have found out about it, plus the two others is from a leak inside the NSA. I know you know about Barayev and Umarov because you've been part of it since the start. But I want to know about Melikov."

"I don't know any Melikov."

"The paper trail says different."

"The paper trail lies."

Bald stopped and turned to look at the mirror. A voice came through his earpiece. "Nothing unusual here. He could be telling the truth."

The NSA man turned back and watched Thomas. It was a long lingering stare which emanated from a deadpan face. Bald waited a little longer watching the man's eyes. Then he asked, "How did this money get into your bank account?"

"I don't know."

"You gave Melikov information, and he paid you for it. Why?"

"I don't know."

"So, you admit you gave him the information?"

"No."

"You just admitted he paid you for it."

"No. I didn't. I don't know how it got there."

"Melikov paid you for the information you gave him."

"I didn't give him any information."

"Yes, you did."

"No, I didn't."

"The paper trail says different. It tells me that you told him where to find the nuclear weapons."

Sweat was starting to appear on Thomas' face. "I don't know anything about it."

"Yes, you do."

"No, I don't."

"Yes, you do."

"No, I ∙on't!"

Bald paused. He waited for the voice in his head to stop and then asked, "What does he have planned?"

"I don't know."

"There you go again, admitting that you told Melikov about the nuclear devices."

"No, I didn't."

"What's he got planned?"

"Who?"

"Melikov."

"I don't know."

"He paid you for information but didn't tell you what he was going to do with it."

"No."

"No what?"

"No everything."

Bald shook his head. "I can do this all day, Brett. Might as well just tell me what you know now because we will get to the truth."

Thomas leaned forward. "I'm telling you, I don't know anything."

Bald got up suddenly from his seat and walked out the door without so much as a word. He returned to the room next door where Miller was now waiting for him. "What do you make of it?"

Miller stared through the two-way mirror; his gaze unwavering. "All the telemetry says he's telling the truth."

"Uh-huh. He just might be."

"But we can't take the chance that he isn't. Push him harder, Scott. Shake his tree and see what falls out. If he is telling the truth, we'll clean up that mess after."

"Yes, sir."

CHAPTER FOURTEEN

Chandigarh, India

They were dressed in black. Even their tactical vests. Across the darkened street sat a two-story house with windows lit by lights from the inside. The SUV they were using was black and would be destroyed once they were done with it.

"As soon as we approach the house, Chunk, you take out that streetlight, Jones, you've got the security camera outside the door. Block, you've got the breaching charge ready to go?"

"Yes, ma'am."

General Mary Thurston dropped the magazine out of her MP5SD out of habit, rechecking everything before replacing it. Beside her sat Sam Jones from the office of military intelligence. He was a solid man in his mid-thirties who'd been a field agent for five years. Before that, he'd been a Ranger. The other two sat in the back: Chunk and Block. Not their real names, of course, but they were the handles the two Delta men went by. And, as their names suggested, they were big men who wore long beards and tight T-shirts.

All three were armed the same as Thurston. MP5SDs, SIG M17s, and each had at least one M84 Flashbang.

The general turned in her seat so she could see all three specialists. "Put them all down. We get in and out with our package. If he's non-ambulatory, then we do what we can. Get him to the evac zone and out of the country. Us with him."

"What about any intel we find?" Block asked.

"No. Just the package."

"Do you read me, Bravo?" Swift's voice came over her comms.

"Talk to me, Slick."

"Ma'am, there are six heat signatures inside. Three downstairs and three more upstairs. Two are moving about up there while one is stationary. I'd say that's our boy."

"Are you ready?"

"When you are, ma'am."

Thurston pulled the balaclava down over her head, so her face was covered. A move which the others imitated. "Let's do it."

They left the vehicle and moved with the fluid movements of a well-oiled machine. Normally Thurston would have had a team around the back to cut off any chance of escape but not this time.

They started across the street. "Chunk," the general said in a low voice.

From behind her, she heard the Delta man's suppressed MP5 fire, and the streetlight went dark.

They stepped noiselessly up onto the sidewalk, and Jones' MP5 knocked out the camera above the solid wood door. Thurston guessed that the door itself would be lined with some form of metal making it impenetrable. Block moved past her silent, stirring the air with his passage, and up the steps to the stoop. With well-practiced movements set the breaching charge. He backed away and took cover with the others.

"Execute, execute, execute," Thurston said, and Block pressed the trigger to detonate the charge.

The explosion rocked the street, and within moments the team had moved inside, Chunk on point followed by Thurston, then Jones and Block.

"Speak to us, Slick," Thurston said.

"Team One, move past the stairs to the room at the rear of the hallway. Team Two, the second floor is yours."

It was a strange feeling moving past sealed doors to rooms, leaving them uncleared. But Thurston had to trust that Swift knew what he was doing and would guide them through it. Ahead of her, the first shooter appeared. Chunk dropped him with two shots. A second man almost fell over his comrade, and while he was unbalanced, the Delta man stopped his clock.

"Team one, the third man seems to be stationary in the kitchen. I think he's crouched behind a cupboard. Team Two you're about to have company at the top of the stairs."

As if on cue, Thurston heard an MP5 fire from the stairs followed by the thud of a body. Ahead of her Chunk turned the corner and immediately reversed his course. The rattle of gunfire from within plastered the wall opposite the doorway with bullet holes. Those that missed the doorway blew through the paper-thin kitchen wall and sprayed chunks of dust and drywall across the narrow hallway.

Thurston was sure she saw a bullet pluck at Chunk's pant leg, but the big man didn't seem to register its passage. Instead, he turned the corner and fired three times. "Tango down," he said in a deep voice before moving forward again.

At the top of the stairs, Jones stepped over the fallen ATS shooter and almost ran headlong into the second. The Indian tried to bring his weapon to bear to shoot him, but Jones was too quick, and he pushed the man's sidearm down which sent three fast shots hammering into the floor at his feet. The ex-Ranger brought his head forward, bringing his forehead swiftly into contact with the bridge of the Indian's nose with a loud crunch. The man cried out in pain and clawed his fingers toward Jones' throat in desperation.

Using all his strength, Jones shoved his attacker away, the Indian stumbling as his legs lost footing and he fell to the floor.

Block pushed past Jones and shot the fallen ATS man through the face. Without hesitating, the Delta man stepped over the corpse. "Where's our package?" he growled.

"There should be a door on your right."

"Got it. Stand by."

Block approached the door and found it unlocked. After turning the handle, he pushed the door gently then peered around the opening and saw a man tied to a chair in the center of the room. Teller looked up to see the newcomer, and the Delta man noted the battered state of the master sergeant's face; covered in bruises and dried blood, one eye was shut, and his lips split and puffy.

"Who are you?" Teller mumbled.

"The cavalry, Buddy. We're the cavalry."

Jones appeared in the doorway. "Is that our man? Are you Master Sergeant Pete Teller?"

"That's me."

"Then you're the man we're here for."

"Who sent you?"

"I did, Master Sergeant."

Teller looked beyond the two men to where Thurston stood in the doorway, her balaclava removed.

Relief flooded through him, and he said, "Good to see you, Ma'am."

"You too, Pete. Can you walk?"

"I'll run if you need me to."

"Let's hope it doesn't come to that. Get him up and out to the SUV." Thurston watched as they released him from his bonds, then helped him to his feet. They supported him by his arms and left the room. She then said into her comms, "Zero? Bravo. Copy?"

"Copy."

"We've got the package. I say again, we've got our package. We're on our way home."

"Copy, Bravo. That's good news. I'll let your ride know you're on your way."

"Thanks, Luis. Bravo, out."

They helped Teller slowly down the stairs and out into the street. Assisting him into the SUV, they secured him first then climbed in too. Jones took his place behind the wheel and started the engine. A couple of heartbeats later, they were gone.

National Security Agency, Fort Meade, Maryland

Brett Thomas was wet with sweat. They'd turned the heat up two hours before, and Bald had questioned him relentlessly.

"Let's go back to the beginning, Brett," Bald said. "How do you know Melikov?"

"I don't. I didn't the last time you asked, and I don't now."

"Why did he pay you then?"

"He didn't."

"Are you sure about that?"

"Yes."

"Ask him if there is anyone who has access to his computer?"

"Does ant one have access to your computer?"

"Everyone in the office. But they don't know my passwords."

"Are you sure?"

There was uncertainty in his eyes.

"What is it?" Bald asked him.

"Nothing. No, there's no way that someone knows my passwords."

Bald studied his face. "There is, isn't there? Who are you screwing from the office?"

Thomas' expression changed, and Bald knew he was onto something. "Who, damn it?"

"Ruth," he replied, his shoulders slumped.

"Ruth Baker?"

"Yes."

Bald turned and looked toward the mirror. On the other side, Miller said to the man closest to him, "Find her."

"How did she get your password?" Bald asked.

"I don't know; I didn't give it to her."

"But she got access to it somehow. I bet you accessed your work computer from home, didn't you? And she was there. You took her home and fucked her and fucked up! She waited until you'd accessed your work computer and then distracted you. Once you were done, instead of pillow talk, she made an excuse to leave the room and set you up perfectly. How long have you two been bumping uglies between the sheets? My guess is it would have started – oh, I don't know – just before the Chechen attacked the teams with the suitcases. And the last time was last night when she left the paper trail for us to find. Fucking moron."

"I thought she liked me," Thomas mumbled. It was almost pathetic.

Bald left the room and went next door. He looked at Miller and said, "I was right."

"Yes, you were."

"Is she still here?"

"As far as we know."

"You want me to interrogate her."

"No. I'll do it. Take a break. I'll see if I can find out if she knows where Melikov is."

"Should I inform Ferrero we found our leak?"

Miller thought for a moment. "Yes."

After he got off the phone, he said to Miller, "You're not going to believe this. They've linked Melikov to the Chechens too."

"And they didn't tell us," Miller theorized, "because of our leak."

"Yes. But that's not all. They think they know where he is. They're sending in a team to snatch him."

"What? Where is he?"

"Grozny. I guess they figure he'll have the answers we all need."

"Let's hope so."

———————

Kandahar, Afghanistan

"I have some good news before we get started," Ferrero said as he addressed the team. "General Thurston was able to secure the release of Pete Teller."

There was a cheer from them all, and Axe asked, "Did they do it willingly, Luis?"

"Not hardly."

"At least he'll be on his way home."

"He'll join Traynor at Ramstein to get checked out."

"Is the doc there?"

"Yes, she is. She said to tell you that Traynor is making progress."

"Thanks to General Jones," Kane added. Then, "What's the news on Scimitar?"

"We should know more in a couple of hours. Last report had them not far from home base."

"At least things are starting to go our way."

Ferrero nodded. "Let's get this briefing over and done with."

The big screen lit up with a picture of what used to be a ten-floor office complex. Part of it had collapsed while the rest was damaged beyond repair. Smaller apartment blocks were spread out in the vicinity while other buildings, not so lucky, were just piles of indeterminate rubble. The leftovers of the Second Chechen War.

What had once been streets were now just debris-strewn trails traversed only by vehicles game enough to brave the unexploded ordnance. Trees were nothing more than sticks with some branches, having never recovered from being stripped at the height of the fighting in Grozny. However, the grass in the picture was more than visible. Down at the bottom right of the picture appeared to be a building with no roof, but the interior walls were visible.

"This building in the center is what used to be Melikov Industries," Ferrero started.

"*The* Melikov?" Brick asked.

"Yes. *The* Melikov. Believe it or not, before the war, Melikov was a successful businessman. But when the Russians came knocking in ninety-nine, he formed his own militia. From two thousand, after his militia was about all wiped out, he set up an insurgent network which took the war into Moscow itself. At one point over the years, there were whispers he was trying to get his hands on a nuclear weapon. Now, it would seem that he's done it."

"He's in there somewhere?" Kane asked.

"Not in, under. Throughout the first and second war, the Chechens built a tunnel system under the city much as the Vietnamese did in the Vietnam war. Although most of it has been sealed up as the city was rebuilt, there are still some sections that remain open and are being utilized."

"I can see it now," Axe grumbled. "We're walking into the rabbit warren of death."

"Aren't we a cheery one?" Cara commented.

"Expect the worst, hope for the best, ma'am."

"How many men does Melikov have?" Arenas asked Ferrero.

"No idea. We assume maybe twenty. He's certain to have some form of bodyguard."

Brick leaned forward in his seat. "Wait, Slick, can you zoom in on the side of that office building?"

The picture on the screen grew larger. Brick nodded. "Is that what I think it is?"

"Looks like our friend Melikov is an ISIS supporter," Kane said.

"Good, we can clean his clock," Axe growled.

"No!" Ferrero snapped. "Melikov gets taken alive so we can question him. Understood?"

"Are you expecting to find the nuke on-site?" Cara asked.

"It's not likely. I believe it'll be in transit to Russia."

"You sound like you're sure about that," Kane said.

"It's the most logical destination given the history. I just hope we can find it before they blow it. Melikov is our best chance to find it before that happens."

"Do we get a guardian angel for this rip down-range?" Kane asked.

Ferrero smiled. "Of course. You're getting a new toy for this op. An Avenger complete with two Hellfires and two five-hundred-pound GBU-38 JDAMs. I love technical terms. For those of you unfamiliar with this UAV it has a ceiling of fifteen thousand meters and a lifespan of eighteen hours. It also has a turbofan powerplant. It's new, it's cutting edge, and we'd best not fuck it up."

Kane looked at Reynolds. "Are you flying this thing?"

She shook her head. "I'm flying second seat on this one. Learning on the job. I know the pilot. You'll be in good hands."

"Good enough for me."

"We'll run everything from here," Ferrero continued. "There will be no QRF, just the Avenger. Once you have your HVT, you call for extract. Admiral Joseph has one of his toys on standby."

A picture popped up on the screen of a flat area cleared of rubble, big enough for a helicopter to touch down. "This is your extract LZ. If it is too hot, then there is another, four kilometers to the west."

Another picture, this time of a park.

"And if that's compromised?" Axe asked.

"Then you run like hell and don't look back," Ferrero said, his face grim. "Get yourselves squared away. Any other questions, come see me."

They dispersed and Kane, with the others, went along to the armory to kit up. Axe picked up an attachable M320 grenade launcher. "I'm taking one of these. Just in case."

Kane nodded. He looked at Cara. "Did you see anything you liked in that shot on the screen?"

Cara picked up a laptop and hit the keys she required. She waited a few moments, and the picture they'd seen in the briefing appeared. She scanned it closely and touched the screen. "There."

The building Cara pointed out was all but destroyed. Only the shell remained. It was about two hundred meters from the target building. "It will give me a clear field of fire. Plus, if anything happens, I'll be able to rain hell down from above on anything that needs it."

Kane nodded. "Everyone pack a couple of grenades each plus one flashbang, just in case. I want NVGs, suppressors, armor plates front and back. And take your KA-Bars. We need to keep this as quiet as possible. Brick, pack the bare essentials, and no more. Gear up."

CHAPTER FIFTEEN

Xinjiang Autonomous Region, China

From amongst the rocks, Hunt stared down from the rocky ridge at the border post where at least thirty Chinese soldiers stood guard. The team was tired, having been on the move non-stop for the past few days. Rucker carried the suitcase nuke; each man took turns.

"That could be an issue," Hunt said and passed the field glasses over to Jenkins. "Thicker than fleas on a dog."

Jenkins nodded. "We've got to get around them somehow."

Popeye settled in beside them. "I don't want to rush things along, but you might want to have a look on our six."

They turned and looked. PLA troops were beating the bushes so to speak and putting the squeeze on them. Hammer and anvil stuff. Hunt said, "Nuts in a wringer about now. So close, yet so far."

"If they catch us with that nuke, they'll shoot us on the spot," Jenkins said.

"They'll shoot us anyway. Now, later, it won't matter much."

"Maybe torture us first," Rucker joined in.

A sigh escaped Jenkins' lips. "We need a diversion."

"Couldn't hurt," Hunt agreed.

There was a drawn-out silence. Each man knew that whichever one of them created the diversion for the others to escape, wouldn't be coming home. Jenkins looked at each of his team-mates. "My idea, I'll do it."

Hunt shook his head. "My team, my responsibility."

"Nope. Your team, your responsibility to see that the suitcase gets back into the right hands. It's Rucker's turn to carry it, so that rules him out. And Popeye is a pussy, so, that leaves me."

"You know this is a one-way trip, Gunner?" Hunt reminded him.

He gave his commander a wan smile. "Anything for my brothers, right?"

"We can work something else out, Gunner," Hunt lied.

"No, we can't, Scimitar. Just have a beer for me when you get home."

"Fuck!" Popeye hissed.

"Give me your gun, Pop," Jenkins said, holding out his hand.

Popeye handed over his QBU-88 sniper rifle. "Make good use of her, Gunner."

Jenkins slung his Bullpup over his shoulder and took the rifle. He nodded grimly. "Just make sure you get that thing out of here. Give me a couple of minutes."

He handed Hunt his comms so they couldn't be identified. Then he turned and started to move along the slope.

"All right," Hunt said. "He's giving us a chance. Let's not waste it."

———————

"This is a dumb fucking idea, Gunner," Jenkins admonished himself. "I guess I'll have to put off that father-son baseball game until next time."

Jenkins cursed himself for being a piss poor father. There was a lot of irony in his thoughts. He'd never been there for Marcus; Ellie had left him when the boy was two. Over the next seven years, he'd seen him the sum total of twice.

His heart beat loudly in his ears as he worked his way into position. He found himself a perfect spot on some high ground. Jenkins lay the QBZ-95 beside himself and set up with the sniper rifle. He looked through the scope and sighted the crosshairs onto the first target he saw. He adjusted for the elevation and wind and then lay there. All it required was just a squeeze of the trigger, which would signal the beginning of the end.

Jenkins took a deep breath and then let it out slowly. He said, "Good luck, Scimitar," and squeezed the trigger.

The bullet reached out, and the first Chinese soldier at the border post fell like a stone. Those around him froze, stunned. Jenkins shifted aim and fired once more. A second soldier fell. The Chinese scattered, taking cover. The SEAL left the sniper rifle where it was and turned, taking the QBZ-95 with him. He opened fire with it on the pursuers which had been coming up behind the team. On full auto, the Bullpup burned through the thirty-round magazine in no time. The Chinese soldiers, instead of running for cover, brought up their weapons and concentrated their fire upon Jenkins' position.

Bullets ricocheted off the rocks where the SEAL sheltered. Sharp shards flew through the air, and Jenkins felt the back of his hand burn as one sliced at the exposed skin. He ignored it and rolled onto his side. He dropped out the magazine and slapped another home as he felt the heat of another close round which burned through the air close to his face.

Jenkins turned again and settled in with the sniper rifle. The soldiers that had been placed at the border were now advancing on his position. The QBU-88 slammed back into his shoulder.

Once.

Twice.

Both times men dropped.

Turn, fire again.

Teeth clenched, keep going, your buddies depend upon you.

Fuck!

The first bullet hit him down low in the side. It tore through material and flesh and hurt like a bitch. Jenkins picked up the smaller weapon and opened fire again.

It was the second bullet which hurt. Burned deep and Jenkins felt it do irreparable damage. "Damn it."

He felt the urge to cough, and a gurgle escaped with it. His lungs were filling with blood. Another bullet punched into his leg and brought forth a stifled cry of pain. "Christ."

The QBZ-95 ran dry, and he reached down to get another magazine. He was starting to feel tired. Very tired.

Jenkins rolled over onto his back and looked up at the sky. His vision blurred and then cleared. For a moment, he thought his ears were playing tricks on him. A dark shadow flitted across the sky and then disappeared.

The SEAL's eyes closed. He was so tired.

———

"What the hell?" Rucker said in wonderment as the

helicopter swooped low overhead. "That ain't one of theirs."

"Keep moving," Hunt ordered realizing that the unmarked bird would act as a further distraction.

"I thought they said they weren't coming for us?" Popeye said.

"At this time, I don't care."

"Alpha One? This is Eagle One, copy?"

"Copy, Eagle One."

"We thought you might need a ride, over."

"Better late than never, Eagle One."

"Just tell us where you want us."

"To my west, there is a low patch of ground. There will do."

"Copy. You've got a ten-second window. After that, you can walk home."

"We'll be there."

"Roger that, Eagle One inbound."

Hunt looked at Rucker and Popeye. "Let's go. Head down, ass up, and run like hell."

They broke cover and ran toward the depression. Suddenly the SEAL became aware of bullets flying all around him. "Why don't that helo shoot at these bastards?" Popeye cursed out loud.

"Maybe they forgot to arm up," Rucker panted.

"I bet they're army dick wads."

"Shut up and run."

The helicopter came in and flared ready to touch down. Behind him, Hunt heard Popeye cry out, and when he looked back, he saw his man down on the ground clutching at his leg. Hunt stopped and went back for his sniper. He dragged him to his feet and snapped, "Push through it, Squid."

"Fuck you."

With his arm draped over Hunt's shoulder, Popeye kept up a lumbering run. By the time they dropped down into the depression, Rucker was about at the helicopter. "Come on, Pop, we're almost there."

Then they were. The rotor wash blasted them as they approached the doorway. A hand reached out and hauled Popeye aboard. Another reached out for Hunt. He took it and looked up. It was Rear-Admiral Joseph, dressed in BDUs. "Where's your other man?"

Hunt just shook his head.

The helicopter lifted off and flew low toward the border.

———

Barkley St, Fort Meade, Maryland

There were five black SUVs which pulled up in the quiet suburban street. Armed men wearing tactical gear poured from each one transforming the picturesque morning into something resembling a war zone.

A commanding officer barked out orders, and the shooters moved swiftly in three teams. One moved toward the front door of the white house while the other two moved left and right, circling around the back of the house.

As soon as they were in the position they breached, setting in motion a chain of cataclysmic events that ended in a giant orange fireball which rose above the normally serene neighborhood.

Grozny, Chechnya

The team picked their way through the debris field with careful precision. Their NVGs painted the destroyed landscape green, making it easier to see through the blackness. Kane pressed the talk button on his comms and said, "Zero? Reaper One. We're passing Charlie and moving to Peanuts."

"Copy, Reaper One."

The team kept on, gutted structures looming over them like giant sentinels. Up on point, Arenas suddenly stopped and took a knee. "Reaper, we've got movement up ahead."

"On my way. The rest of you keep your eyes peeled."

They set up a small perimeter while Kane moved silently forward. He settled beside Arenas and asked, "What have you got?"

"Looks like a patrol," he whispered. "Out there at

about one o'clock."

Kane studied the terrain and saw the figures making their way toward them. Two men armed with automatic weapons he surmised. "I have them."

"What do you want to do?"

"We'll let them walk on by," Kane told him. "Reaper One to all elements. Take cover. Make yourselves small."

They all broke squelch in reply. Kane said to Arenas, "Let's go."

The team had been on the ground for two hours and planned on being in place for long enough to observe their target before going in. The insertion had gone off without a hitch.

"Bravo One, how's that Avenger coming along?"

"It'll be on station in five minutes, Reaper One."

"Next time get one that works."

"Hearing you, Lima Charlie," Reynolds replied. "It is a prototype."

The Chechens approached. They walked past the shell of a two-floor apartment block toward where the team was hunkered down. As they grew closer, their voices became louder. One of them laughed at something the other one said, and then they turned the corner of an almost invisible street and walked away.

"Axe, Brick, see where they go. We'll wait here for you. Cara, on me."

"Copy that."

Cara appeared out of the darkness. "What's up?"

"Your hide is about two hundred meters along this street. We'll hole up there for a while and then move in once the Avenger is in position. With its thermal camera hopefully, it might be able to help see what's in hell."

Axe and Brick arrived back and reported that the roving patrol disappeared amidst the rubble a hundred meters further on. "OK," Kane said. "Let's move."

They reached the remains of the shelled-out building and took up positions on the bottom floor. A concrete internal staircase led up to what was left of the third floor where Cara would set up. They'd also secured a rappelling rope and left it looped so it wasn't anywhere it could be seen. Just in case Cara was cut off from her primary escape route.

"Reaper One? Bravo One. Copy?"

"Copy, Bravo one."

"Our air asset is now on station."

"All right. Light her up and tell me what you see."

"Roger that."

After a long silence, Reynolds came back to him and said, "Reaper, you're not going to like this. I'm getting multiple heat signatures below ground plus another four to your east about four-hundred meters."

"Roving patrol?"

"Nope, I've accounted for those. These are stationary in another bombed-out building."

"Best guess, Bravo One?"

"OK. Best guess is that they're watching the same target."

Kane thought for a moment before an idea formed. "Russians?"

"Good possibility. Like I said, you aren't going to like it."

"Any sign of others?"

"No."

"Good chance that they are an advanced Spetsnaz team?"

"Very good chance, Reaper."

"Shit," Kane cursed. "Bravo Four, have you found a hole for us to crawl into yet?"

"I think so, Reaper. Northeast corner of the building. I've been looking over the image that Brooke just brought up, and the only ones who aren't moving are those stationed there. My guess is that they are stationary security."

"Let's hope so," Kane acknowledged. "I guess we'll find out."

"Another thing, Reaper One. I just picked up a burst of traffic over a secure link," Swift chuckled. "Funny, isn't it? Secure link. The Russians really need to update their shit. Your friends just sent a flash message out to whoever is communicating with them."

"Were you able to figure out what they said?"

Kane asked.

"Something about "narushitel"."

"What's that mean?"

"Intruder."

"I guess that means they know we are here."

"Quite possible."

"We need to go. Now. Carlos, stay with Cara just in case these Russians try something."

"Roger that, amigo."

"Brick. Axe. On me. Time to go to work."

———————

Using hand signals, Kane indicated he was about to breach. He broke squelch and Reynolds said over her comms, "The two guards should be just around the corner from you."

The three Team Reaper shooters had approached the guard post on its blindside. The post itself was inside what had once been the entrance alcove of the shattered structure. Kane brought up the suppressed M17 and stepped around the bullet marked wall and exposed himself.

The handgun bucked in his hand twice. The first two bullets punched into the chest of the sentry closest to him. Then Kane shifted his aim and squeezed the trigger twice more with the same result.

"Two tangos down."

Brick and Axe swept around the corner and

dragged the two dead men out of the way and hid their bodies. Kane opened the door where the two men had been standing. It made a creaking sound, and he stopped, holding his breath. He listened intently for a moment and said to Reynolds, "We're going in."

Kane squeezed through the opening to encounter a set of crude steps before him which dropped away sharply. "I've got stairs going down."

His first few steps were hesitant before he kept on until he reached the bottom. The unlit tunnel moved directly away from him toward a solid concrete wall. Kane walked slowly forward; the 416 slung while he kept the suppressed M17 at eye level. Behind him, he heard the other two following, their breaths sounding loud in the confined space.

He reached the turn and went right. In his ear, he heard Reynolds say, "The next tangos will be somewhere to your left. About ten meters."

"I've got a turn ahead of me," Kane whispered back.

He peered around the corner and saw a door at the end of the hallway. Beneath it shone a light. He edged back around and said to Brick and Axe. "We've got a door at the end of the hallway with a light showing under it. Axe, rear security. Brick and I will clear it."

"Copy that."

"Bravo One, how many tangos in this room?"

"Three."

"Copy," he replied, then, "Try not to kill Melikov if he's in there."

"Can't promise that."

Although they were highly trained, Kane knew that there would be no time to look and see if their HVT was there inside the room. As soon as they breached, they would have to kill quickly and efficiently, for if they hesitated, they could be killed themselves.

Normally a flashbang would be used to disorient whoever was beyond the door. But that would alert the rest to their presence. As it was there was every chance a tango would get off a shot.

Kane put the M17 away and unslung his 416. He flicked the safety selector around to semi. He raised it to his shoulder, and behind him, Brick did the same. Suddenly he stopped. The underground passage turned to his right. Kane pressed his talk button and said in a soft voice, "Axe, get up here."

The big man broke squelch and moved up behind the two men. Using hand signals, Kane told Axe to watch the passage while he and Brick prepared to breach. The Team Reaper leader reached out and tried the doorknob. It turned, and the door opened a crack.

Kane lifted his NVGs and thrust it open. He stepped through into the bright light and swept the room to his left as he walked forward. The 416 spat muted fire, and the tango who appeared in front of

Kane dropped without a sound.

Behind him, Brick did the same only he was sweeping the room to his right. As silent as his friend, the second Chechen dropped to the cold hard floor.

But that still left one, and both suppressed gun muzzles targeted the remaining man at the same time. Both weapons fired in sync and the final man died just as silently as the others.

With the room cleared they checked to make sure the fallen were indeed dead nor Melikov. With that done, they went back outside, closed the door, and plunged the passage into darkness once more.

"Zero? Reaper One. We've made contact. Have five tangos down, none of them are Melikov, over."

"Copy, Reaper One."

"Reaper One, be advised that there are two more tangos at your twelve o'clock."

Kane froze. Then through the green haze, he made out the next doorway. He walked forward again, and as he grew closer, he saw the light shining under the door. Once more, the NVGs went up. He reached out to test the doorknob, and as soon as he touched it, the door in front of him seemed to explode outward as a hailstorm of bullets burst through it.

CHAPTER SIXTEEN

Grozny, Chechnya

"Shit! Fuck!" Kane cursed as he pinned himself against the concrete wall to make himself as small a target as possible.

On the other side of the door, automatic gunfire rattled and shredded the thin obstruction. Kane said, "Zero, we're taking heavy fire. I say again, we're taking heavy fire."

Behind Kane, Axe opened fire with his 416 on full auto. He blew a full magazine through the door, hoping to suppress the fire from within. A cry of, "Changing!" signaled that the magazine was empty, and it was time for Brick to continue the hail of lead.

Once he was empty, it seemed as though the bullets had stopped coming. Kane flicked up this NVGs and pulled the pin on one of his grenades. He called, "Frag out!" and poked it through the hole which had been created in the door and dropped to the floor.

A desperate "No!" came echoing throughout the passage from Brick. He knew what it was about. If Melikov was on the other side of the shattered door, then there was a good chance he would be killed. But if whoever was on the other side got the chance to open fire then he and his team were in a funnel. Besides, he was taking a guess that Melikov wasn't the bravest of the brave and that he would be running by now, hiding.

With a loud CRUMP! the grenade exploded and blew apart what was left of the door, filling the passage with a flood of heat, dust, and debris. Kane came up off the floor, his ears ringing. He raised the 416 and pushed through into the room. It looked to be a kind of meeting room with tables and chairs that were piles of matchwood. On the west wall, there looked to be what was once a map. Both shooters were dead. "Room clear!"

"I'll check to see if one of them is Melikov," Axe said.

"He's not here," Kane told him.

"How do you know?"

"He's prone to survival. He won't have stayed."

"Heads up, Reaper One," Reynolds said over his comms. "There is inbound traffic from the north, two trucks, and our Russian friends are on the move."

"I've got them," Cara said. "Should I engage?"

Kane said, "Not the Russians, keep an eye on them. The others, if they turn out to be the bad guys, weapons hot, Reaper two,"

"Copy."

"Damn it, Reaper, you have six tangos closing on your position from your east and south."

"Roger that, Bravo One," Kane replied and turned to Axe. "Get the lights."

Axe looked up automatically and saw that the light there was already shattered. "What the fuck?" Then it registered for the first time. The lights were at floor level in the lower part of the walls. He quickly shot them out, condemning the room to darkness. The three of them pulled down their NVGs and waited for death to knock.

"Carlos keep an eye on Ivan."

"Yes, ma'am."

Cara shifted her gaze and watched the two trucks bounce along the rough debris-lined street. Headlights bounced wildly as the lead truck hit a hole at speed. "These guys are in a hurry."

"Cara, the Russians are taking up ambush positions."

"We know they aren't theirs at least," she said. "Zero, the Russians are moving to ambush the two trucks."

"Copy, Reaper Two. I suggest they are there for the same reason we are. Although I'd say that they aren't privy to the intelligence we have. Melikov must not fall into their hands. If he does, we'll never get the information that we need, and a lot of people will die."

"Are you telling me to kill the Russians, Zero?"

"I'm saying Melikov mustn't fall into their hands."

"Roger, Zero."

She thought for a moment and said to Arenas, "Carlos, we need to keep the Russians busy."

"How are we going to do that?"

"Like this," she said and shot out the front window on the first truck.

The vehicle shuddered to a stop, and the one following it almost ran into it from behind. Instantly men were discharged from the covered rear. They were all armed and looking for targets.

Taken by surprise at what had just happened, the Russian element was slow to respond. However, once they had gathered themselves, they engaged without prejudice and started killing the Chechens out of hand.

"That'll keep them busy. Come on, we need to move."

———

Starshina Leonid Pavlov cursed out loud at the situation he and his men found themselves in. There were other forces on the ground compromising their operation to capture Melikov, and it appeared that their operation had all gone to *er'mo*.

"Fucking assholes," he swore again as he fired his AK-15 at the nearest Chechen terrorist. "Gennadi, we must push forward before Melikov can get away."

The man next to him snapped, "Be my fucking guest."

Pavlov knew that their backup team wasn't going to arrive in time to help them. They had been forced to bivouac outside of Grozny on a farm. They were still ten minutes away. It was bullshit, but it was all they'd had at the time. If Melikov had gotten wind of their presence, he would have disappeared again.

"Christ on a crutch," Pavlov snarled and came to his feet. He roared at his men, "Come on, you useless bunch of motherless whores! Today we die for Mother Russia!"

The three others followed his lead. They picked out their targets with methodical precision. To Pavlov's left Andrey Kozlov fell forward with a grunt. He was a big man and hit the ground with a solid thump. Ignoring his fallen comrade, Pavlov continued shooting until his magazine went dry. Then he dropped it out with meticulous ease and slapped another one home.

"Gennadi, the second truck!"

Pavlov's second in command shifted his direction of advance toward the second vehicle. The Chechens returned fire, but it was more spray and pray than anything else. However, they got lucky again. Gennadi called out, "Yuri is fallen, Leonid!"

"Keep going! Argh—"

A bullet punched into the Russian's left shoulder, and he fell to his knee. A shadow loomed in front of him. A weapon came up, and in that instant, Pavlov realized he was about to die. Instead of pulling the trigger, the Chechen died on his feet as a 7.62 NATO round blew through his brain.

———

A pang of guilt tugged at Cara's heart when she saw the second Russian fall. She didn't know why but there it was. It was then she made the decision to help out. So, when the Chechen raised his weapon to kill a third Russian operator, she killed him before he could fire.

"Carlos, give the Russians some cover."

"Yes, ma'am."

The Mexican opened fire with his suppressed 416. Within a matter of seconds, the terrorists realized their dire predicament, and they started to fall back. Suddenly the fire started to die away and then petered out altogether.

Cara and Arenas moved forward. The fallen Russian rose from his knee and turned his weapon on them. "Who the fuck are you?" he asked harshly.

"Easy, big man," Cara said. "You don't want to bite off more than you can chew."

"You do not belong here," Pavlov snarled. "Your

presence got my men killed."

"In a way," Cara allowed. "But right at this minute, I have men engaged underground."

"What are they doing? They are ruining our operation."

"Are you after Melikov?"

"Yes."

"So are we."

"You cannot have him."

"Finders keepers, my friend."

"Reaper Two, you have more vehicles incoming."

Cara's expression changed. "How many, Bravo One?"

"Three. They look like more Russians."

Cara looked at Pavlov and realized what the burst of traffic had been earlier. It was Pavlov calling them in. "Your friends are about to arrive," she said to the sergeant.

Pavlov just nodded.

Cara weighed up what to do next. She said into her comms, "Zero, copy?"

"Copy, Reaper Two."

"Three and I will be off comms for a bit. Will let you know when we're back up."

"What's going on, Cara?"

"Reaper Two, out."

"Ca—"

"Carlos put your weapon down." As she said it, she lay the CSASS at her feet.

Pavlov looked at her curiously. "What are you doing?"

"Trying to stop a nuclear weapon from going off."

———————

The rattle of gunfire in the confined space almost made Kane feel like his head would explode. Bullets ricocheted off the dense concrete walls, with the misshapen hunks of lead turning into unpredictable missiles.

Kane put a slug into the chest of a shooter whose large frame filled the doorway. The man fell forward, like a great tree falling, across one of his comrades who were already there. To Kane's right Axe made short work of another shooter.

Instantly, everything went quiet. Apart from the ringing in their ears, that is. Kane said, "Clear."

"Me too," said Axe sounding like he was miles away.

"Let's keep moving."

They entered the hallway, which traveled east. It turned to the right twenty meters further along and then came to another halt when it disappeared beyond yet another door. This one, however, was different. It was steel. Not unlike a bulkhead hatch on a ship.

"Axe, get a look at this."

The big man came forward. "Looks solid, Reaper."

"Reckon you can fix it with a breaching charge?"

"I'll give it a go. It's all about placement. You reck-on he's behind here?"

"I guess we're about to find out."

———————

The three vehicles slid to a stop. Out of the lead, Iveco LMV jumped a tall man dressed in full tactical gear and carrying an AK-15 just as Pavlov and his men had been. As he walked toward them, the men behind him began setting up a perimeter. "Pavlov, what is happening?" he demanded.

"It is *trakhal*," Pavlov spat.

"Explain."

"Fucking Americans."

The officer shifted his gaze. "You have one minute to tell me who you are before I kill you for interfering in an ongoing operation."

"Reaper Two, Worldwide Drug Initiative."

"Who?"

"Which part didn't you get, asshole?"

"My name is Captain Dimitri Vasilev. I will be addressed as such."

"OK."

"Answer the question," Pavlov snapped.

"I already did, we're from the WDI."

"And what is it you actually do?" Vasilev asked.

"I'm not really sure at the moment. Mostly we take assholes off the map, but at the moment we're trying to stop an asshole from taking us off the map."

"You talk in circles."

"Sometimes."

"What do you want with Melikov?"

"We're hoping he will answer some questions for us."

"He belongs to us. We will take him back to Russia for interrogation."

Cara shrugged. "Only if you get him first."

"What do you mean?"

Suddenly there was a commotion at the edge of the Russian perimeter, and then Kane and the others appeared pushing a gray-haired man along in front of them with his hands cable-tied behind his back. Cara turned her gaze back to Vasilev and said, "Snap."

———

The charge had worked a treat, and Kane, Axe, and Brick had breached the door. On the other side of they found a large open plan living quarters completely finished to a high level of comfort.

They'd also found Melikov there with his personal bodyguards; three men armed with handguns who put themselves between their boss and the three Team Reaper operators. The rattle of suppressed gunfire had taken care of the issue, and the Chechens fell to the floor.

Kane had hurried forward; his 416 pointed straight at the gray-haired man before him. "Are you Usman Melikov?"

The man raised his hands but didn't say a word. Maybe his hearing had been affected by the blast. "Are you Usman Melikov?" Kane asked louder as he took the man's hands and tied them behind his back.

"Yes," Melikov answered. "Who are you?"

"We're the guys who are taking you out of here."

"I'm not going anywhere with you," he snarled.

"We could leave you here for the Russians, I guess," Kane surmised. "They're out there watching you."

A flash of alarm registered in the killer's eyes before disappearing just as quick. "Thought so," Kane said.

"Zero, we've got the package. We're coming out."

"Reaper One, be aware that the Russians are on-site and Reaper two has gone off comms."

"Copy, Zero. We'll go and say hello."

They escorted Melikov back through to the exit and outside. Then they circled the building until they ran into the Russian perimeter.

"Got yourself a problem here, Cara?" Kane asked as they closed in on the group.

"The captain and I were just talking about our prisoner."

"You will hand him over to us this minute," Vasilev demanded.

"No, I don't believe I will," Kane replied. "You see, we need to question him."

The Spetsnaz captain waved his hand and said, "Then we will take him."

Suddenly weapons were pointed in all directions. Friend and foe alike. Kane remained calm and shook his head. "I can't let that happen. We really need to question him. If you don't let us go, then I will have to unleash the hand of God upon you."

The Russian chuckled in disbelief. "Typical American bullshit."

Kane nodded and smiled back. "Bravo One."

"On its way, Reaper One."

Traveling at over sixteen hundred kilometers per hour, the Hellfire missile was indeed the hand of God. A short screech announced its arrival just before impacting with an orange flash and a loud roar, about one hundred meters from their position.

The startled Russians looked around, but Kane and the others were unfazed. He said to Vasilev, "Here's what is going to happen. We're going to take our friend here and question him. After which we'll be able to save countless lives from a nuclear explosion."

"What?" Vasilev snapped.

"You heard me. Somewhere out there are some of his friends with a suitcase nuke. Now given he's a Chechen and how much he hates you lot, I'd say that it's a good chance that it could be headed for your backyard."

"More reason for us to –"

"—Let us do what we're going to do."

"If I let you go with this information my superiors will send me to gulag."

"And if you don't, we'll drop a fucking Hellfire on you, asshole," Axe growled. "We're trying to stop a global war here."

"Sir," Pavlov said in a low voice. "Maybe we should let them take him."

"What? No."

"I tell you what," Kane said. "You come with us, and you can be part of the interrogation. Either way, we're wasting time, and there's a nuke out there which could be about to go off."

"You overlook one thing. Chechnya is Russia. You are in my country, and your presence here could be taken as an act of war."

"You really going to go there?" Kane asked. "We're not part of the American military. We're a force which – ah fuck it. We're wasting time. You coming or not?"

"Where?"

"Incirlik Turkey."

After a long deliberation, Vasilev nodded. "I will come with you. Pavlov, take the men with you and let the colonel know what is happening."

"Yes, sir."

"Well comrade, what do I call you?" Vasilev asked Kane.

"They call me Reaper."

CHAPTER SEVENTEEN

Incirlik, Turkey

By the time they hit the ground in Turkey, there was an entourage awaiting them. From CIA to FSB to NSA and Team Reaper's Bravo element, including Thurston and General Hank Jones.

"Good to see you in one piece," Thurston greeted him with a smile, looking him over to make sure he was.

"You too, ma'am. How's everybody doing?"

Teller's a little roughed up but OK. Traynor has been moved to Ramstein and Teller is there with him."

"Traynor doing OK?"

"He'll be fine. Rosanna is looking after him."

"And you?"

"Never better."

"What happens now?"

"With Melikov?"

"Yes."

"CIA and FSB will question him."

"And while that happens, we wait."

"We've done all we can."

Suddenly Swift appeared. "Ma'am, do you have a moment?"

"Yes."

"Maybe you too, Reaper."

He and Thurston looked curiously at one another then followed the tech into the operations room. "What is it?" Thurston asked.

"You know how I have a habit of not letting things go?"

"Yes."

"Well, there was something that bugged me about all of this. Especially how it all fits together."

"It fits well," Kane pointed out.

"I agree. But only because someone wants it to fit. Let's start at the beginning."

Thurston rolled her eyes. "Do we have to?"

"Colonel Ajeet Khan stole the weapons, took them to Kashmir where they were converted into suitcase nukes where he was going to use them to start a war between Pakistan and India. Something happened, and somehow the Chinese guy was involved, and we know how that went. Enter the Chechens."

"Yes, any day now will be good to reach a point," Kane urged him.

"The NSA analyst feeds information to Melikov, and he puts his teams into action because what terrorist wouldn't want a nuke to play with. They make their play, and they make off with one of the weapons."

"I'm going to sleep, Slick," Thurston growled.

He shifted his gaze to Kane. "What were his living quarters like?"

"Melikov?"

"Yes."

"Nothing great. He was comfortable."

"It would have taken millions to put this together."

"Yes, we traced the money trail back to him."

"But where did he get the money from?"

"What?"

"The man has been living underground for years. Just look at the way he is. He hasn't seen sunlight since forever. If he had the money to put all this together, don't you think that he would be living somewhere else?"

Thurston said, "Are you saying that someone else is backing this whole thing?"

"I am," Swift said with a broad smile.

"Who?"

"The FSB."

"Bullshit," Thurston growled. "Why would the FSB do all this so the Chechens could bomb their own country?"

"Unless the target isn't Russia," Kane said.

"Exactly!" Swift exclaimed.

"But if Russia isn't the target, then what is?" the general asked.

Kane didn't answer. His mind was ticking over like an over-revving machine. "Son of a bitch. What if those Spetsnaz soldiers weren't there on a hunter/killer mission? What if they were babysitting Melikov instead to make sure nothing happened to him until the right time? It would put a lot of things into perspective. FSB supplies the money, Melikov supplies the manpower, and he already has the intelligence."

"But they attacked Melikov's men when they appeared," Thurston pointed out.

"Maybe they attacked them because we were there."

"Why does he get in touch with the FSB when he gets the intel?"

"He didn't. They found him. They already knew where he was. I'll bet that the analyst at the NSA wasn't Chechen. I bet she was an FSB agent."

Swift said, "What if it's not all of the Spetsnaz soldiers? Maybe it is only one man."

"It would explain why the FSB wanted an agent here for the interrogation," Thurston said.

Kane nodded. "And why Vasilev wanted to hold onto him so bad."

"And now the FSB have an agent inside with Melikov."

Suddenly an alarm sounded, and confusion reigned. Kane cursed under his breath then exclaimed, "The interrogation room!"

Both he and Thurston hurried from ops and out into the hallway. Kane had drawn his M17 and was ready to use it. Axe appeared to his right. Kane said, "On me."

They traversed the hallway's many corners until they reach the interrogation cubicle. Kane burst into the room with Axe hot on his hammer. Melikov was face down across a stainless-steel table, his hands still handcuffed to the rail across its center. A hole in his head leaked blood and formed a pool beneath it.

On the floor beside the table was the CIA officer and the man from the NSA. Another man stood over him, a young agent, his fresh-faced appearance now stark white. "What happened?" Kane snapped.

"They shot them."

"Who?"

"The Russians. I was in the observation room. They were asking questions, and then they shot them."

"How did they get weapons in here?" Thurston asked. "Weren't they searched?"

"I don't think so, ma'am."

"Christ," Kane breathed. "Come on, Axe."

The rushed from interrogation and along the hallway in the opposite direction to the way they had arrived.

They almost missed it. The fire door was still open a fraction, and if Axe hadn't glanced down when he did, they would have kept going the way they were headed. And lacking comms they had no use of the internal security system.

"Reaper! Here."

Kane stopped and turned. Axe had pushed the fire door open and was holding his sidearm, up ready to use. Beyond it was another hallway and another door. This one had a sign above it which read: **EXIT**.

They broke out into bright sunshine and had to shield their eyes. They looked left and right and saw no sign of the two men they were after. Kane said, "This way."

The pair started to run towards a C-17 hangar. A massive structure which was built to house a massive plane. They rounded the open door and saw nothing save for a beast of an aircraft.

Kane and Axe separated as they made their way inside. They slowly walked across the wide expanse of the concrete floor toward the rear of the hangar. Axe walked to the left of the C-17 while Kane walked to the right. At the nose of the plane were a couple of doors which led through to some smaller machinery rooms. Overhead was a large machinery gantry.

The hangar was silent. The only sounds Kane could hear were his own breath and the grit under his boots as it crunched on the concrete floor.

He glanced at Axe who had his M17 up at eye

level, then disappeared behind the rear of the plane; its ramp was down which fed up into its cavernous hold. Kane stopped and walked toward the ramp. He placed his left foot on it and then his right. He swept the bay but saw nothing. The only place the two men could have gone was up into the cockpit. Nothing there except certain capture.

Kane stepped back down from the ramp and walked towards the beast's wing. Two huge Pratt & Whitney F117-PW-100 turbofan engines hung down below it. Kane walked under the wing toward the nose of the C-17.

To his left, Axe was standing still, slightly ahead of his position. M17 still raised. The big man paused and looked across at his team leader. He'd seen something. A door was slightly ajar. One with a sign which said: **Keep Closed**.

The two of them moved swiftly forward until they were positioned on either side of the door. Kane looked at his friend and then nodded. Axe eased the door open with his boot, and the air was immediately ripped by a fusillade of gunfire. Bullets hammered into the plane's fuselage, and Axe winced. "There goes any amount of money."

Kane leaned around the doorway and fired. More bullets from within burned through the air. Axe reached into his pocket and pulled out a grenade. "Here!"

Kane looked at him. "Really? You want to let that thing go in here? Do you have any idea what is in that room?"

Axe shrugged and without any thought of his own safety, leaned forward and looked inside. Then, just as casually, leaned back. "Looks like some computers and shit."

His team leader just stared at him.

He stuffed the grenade back in his pocket and said, "Fine. We'll do it your way."

With a guttural growl, Axe replaced the magazine in his handgun with a fresh one and went to work. Before he entered the room, the weapon had already been fired three times. He was using a seventeen round magazine instead of a twenty-one, so he still had fourteen rounds left.

Kane cursed out loud at his friend's recklessness as he disappeared ahead of him. A cry of pain emanated from inside, and Kane moved swiftly to join his friend, concerned that he might be in trouble.

He wasn't. The two Russians lay dead on the floor of the room. Kane looked at Axe and said, "Did you have to kill them both?"

"Seemed like the thing to do."

"Great. Now we have fuck all."

———————

"Not exactly true," Swift said to them.

"Well then, what do you have?" Kane asked him.

"Not a lot. At least we know now that the FSB is behind it."

"No shit, Sherlock," Cara said with a roll of her eyes. "How about you tell us what the target is."

"I don't know that yet."

Thurston and Ferrero looked at each other. Ferrero said, "You think the head of the FSB is at the top of the pyramid on this one?"

"Without a doubt."

"Then we need to work out what to do," Thurston said.

"We could tell the Russian government," Swift suggested.

Ferrero shook his head. "They wouldn't believe it."

"Show them the evidence."

"Who knows how far up the chain this goes," Kane said.

"Which leads us back to having to find that bomb."

"We could always kill him, I guess. Chop the head off the snake."

They all stared at Hank Jones as he entered the room. "Are you serious, sir?" Thurston asked.

"Sure as shit, I am. This son of a bitch needs taking down a peg or two. Normally I wouldn't sanction an op like this, but is there anyone in this room who thinks they can frag his ass?"

"I can," Brick said. It wasn't bragging or anything like that. Just a statement of fact about something the ex-SEAL believed he could do.

"You sure you want to do this?" Thurston asked him.

"Someone has to. The rest of you will be busy finding the last nuke."

Thurston nodded and looked at Jones. The general said, "OK, then. Report to Admiral Joseph. He'll get you into the country."

"Speaking of the admiral, sir," Kane said. "How's Scimitar and the others?"

"He's pissed. He lost a man. No one likes that. But the sun will rise tomorrow, and he'll go downrange again. Just like you lot. Fact of life."

"Yes, sir."

"Now, let's see what we can do about finding these pricks who want to blow shit up."

"I've found them," Swift blurted out to Thurston who sat at a round table drinking black coffee strong enough to stand a horseshoe in.

"Where?" she asked, stopping the cup halfway to her lips.

"England."

"How the hell—"

"Don't ask. All I know is I'm reasonably sure that's where they are."

"Reasonably sure?"

Swift's head danced from side to side. "Maybe eighty percent."

"Eighty percent?"

"OK. Sixty."

"Christ."

"I know they're there, Ma'am. I can feel it."

Thurston nodded. "Sell it to me. And make it damned good."

"The Russians and the Brits have been on bad terms ever since the Novichok incident where the British blamed them for trying to kill the Russian dude, right. It's taken them virtually back to the Cold War. Each side expelled diplomats, spies really, and so did other countries. Anyway, the accusations flew back and forth with the outcome more or less in favor of the Brits. Which meant that Russia lost face in the eyes of the western world."

"You think this is payback?"

"On a grand scale. In three days, there are to be celebrations for the Queen's birthday. There will be people out in their thousands concentrated in a very small area. Not to mention all of those who will be attending from abroad."

"I still haven't heard anything to convince me that they are there."

"I'm telling you they are, ma'am."

She stared at him for a moment, musing briefly then nodding at his certainty, and said, "All right. Get me everything you can. Run every scenario and find every possible place that Barayev and Umarov might hide the damned thing."

"Yes, ma'am."

———————

"Axel, do you know the Queen?"

The question was out of left field, and Axe glanced at Kane. "She called me Axel again."

"She did."

"Now I'm nervous."

"You should be."

"I wish she wouldn't do that."

"Maybe you should ask her why."

"Yeah," Axe said with a nod. "Why, ma'am?"

"You knew the pope, so I thought I'd ask about the queen."

"Well—"

All eyes turned in his direction.

He paused, then said, "What? I can't help it if I know famous people. She said I was a nice young man."

"I don't believe it," Cara commented, shaking her head. "Are there any famous people, perhaps, any minor celebrities that you don't know, by chance?"

"I never met Nelson Mandela. Great man he was."

"I have to ask," Thurston interrupted. "When and where did you meet the queen?"

He looked at the general innocently then gave her his biggest shit-eating grin yet. "Of course, I don't know the queen. Got you all good though, didn't I?"

"Asshole," Thurston hissed, setting the group off

into guffaws of laughter. "Let's get on with this. Our wonder man Slick there has come up with the notion that the Chechens are already in London."

"Based on what?" Kane asked skeptically.

"You don't want to know. I'm telling you, that's where they are, and within the next few days, they will detonate the bomb if they aren't stopped."

"Few days?"

Thurston said, "We believe that they will wait until the queen's birthday to set it off."

"But you still have no proof?"

"No, nothing concrete, yet." The tone of his voice did not convey any disappointment at having nothing firm, as he was convinced that he was on the money and would soon have the evidence.

"Shit."

"You're going to London," Thurston said curtly. "All of us. We need to find this bomb."

"And what if it's not there?"

"Then we might get to stay alive. This is not a democracy; we are all going. Lives depend on it. Gear up, get your shit in order."

CHAPTER EIGHTEEN

Moscow, Russia

Arriving late that night at Lenin Terminal, Brick stepped from the train. Outside, the sky was dark, but the space within the terminal seemed brighter than day, the source of the glow, rows of giant floodlights hovering overhead. The wide concrete platform seemed overly crowded for eleven in the evening, but Brick thought that he may be able to use it to his advantage. He glanced to his right and immediately spotted his tail. A big man dressed smartly in a suit and long coat glanced furtively in his direction. "You'll have to do better than that, asshole," Brick murmured.

Walking forward, he entered the crush of humanity, an almost overpowering combination of smells, some nasty like body odor, cloying perfumes, liquor and halitosis, others nice, hit him as he turned to his left, then began moving with the human wave. He'd managed to travel only about twenty meters when a cell phone started to ring. Frowning, Brick glanced about but did not stop. When it continued to go unanswered, he realized that the sound was emanating from his own coat pocket. The right one; his was in his left. He reached down and felt the hard, vibrating form of another phone. Retrieving it from his jacket, he held it up and stared at it, looking for the caller ID. There was none.

Brick looked around warily before hitting the answer button and raising it up to his ear. The voice on the other end was distinctly British. "Up ahead, you'll see a hallway. Turn into it."

"What?" Brick asked, for no other reason than for want of something to say.

The cell went dead.

The ex-SEAL stared at the cell and then glanced back through the crowd. His tail was still present.

Peering over the heads ahead of him, Brick saw the narrow hallway that had been mentioned by the caller. A sign protruding from the gray painted wall indicated that it led to the restrooms. Upon reaching the hallway, he turned to look around for anyone acting suspicious, however seeing only people coming and going from the bathrooms, and fellow travelers walking the concourse, there was nothing to note. He had even lost sight of his tail.

Turning down the tiled walkway, each step

echoing down the long, enclosed space, he saw three doors going to the bathrooms; women's, men's, and one for the disabled. The ex-SEAL looked back, and once again caught sight, as the man who was following him turned the corner. Brick turned to face him.

To his right, the door of the disabled restroom was opened a crack, and a voice whispered, "Get in here."

Without hesitating, Brick stepped briskly to the door of the small tiled room, entering and closing the heavy barrier behind him with a squeak.

The man on the other side of the door was attired in a black suit and long black coat. Thoughts of old cold war movies that he'd watched as a youngster sprang to mind as he noticed the man screwing a suppressor onto the barrel of a handgun. "Pleased to meet you, Mister Peters. Won't be a moment."

He guided Brick to the center of the room and stood next to the doorway with his weapon raised. The door swung open with the squeak of unlubricated hinges. The covert tail took two steps into the bathroom, and the Brit shot him in the side of the head.

Blood spatter showered the tiled wall, the man's body making a sickening thud as it hit the floor. The Brit stepped forward and unscrewed the suppressor. "Come on, old chap, time to leave."

"What the fuck?"

"Our friend on the floor was FSB. His mission was to kill you."

"How the hell does he know I'm even here?"

"How does one know anything, old boy?"

"Who are you, anyway?" Brick growled.

"Grover, MI6. Come on, no time for chit-chat."

Pocketing the weapon and suppressor, Grover put his head outside the door to make sure things were clear, then stepped into the corridor, Brick close on his heels. They hurried back out into the main part of the station and turned right. "Where are we going?"

"Tatiana Hotel. You have a room booked there under the name of Woodrow Wilson."

"You're shitting me?"

"Not in the slightest. Thought it would be a bit of a laugh."

"Christ."

They emerged from the station and climbed into the back of a Toyota Camry. Without turning around, the driver pulled away from the curb and drove into traffic. The flicker of orange streetlights cast a wan illumination into the rear of the vehicle. Grover produced a large envelope from somewhere and passed it over to Brick. "You'll need these."

Brick opened the envelope and found a passport with his photo but with a false name and some papers. "Everything else you require you'll find in your room. How many days will you need?"

"Once I know his movements, then I'll know."

"Once again, everything regarding that will be in your room."

"Do I have any backup?"

Grover shook his head. "Should you run into any trouble, a preprogrammed number in the cell in your room will connect you. The emergency password is "Gloria". Say it once and then hang up. We'll find you. When the job is done, same thing different code. The password is "Elizabeth". Got it?"

"Got it."

"How you do it is up to you. If you look like getting caught, kill yourself. Anything else would be less than pleasant for both you and the countries involved."

"But mostly for me."

"Yes, quite."

The interior of the Camry went quiet. Buildings flashed by, fronts lit by neon signs, bright light spilling from windows. One block further on, the street corner held a gaggle of scantily clad young women.

"Prostitutes," Grover said. "Run by the Russian Mafia. Most of them aren't even Russian. A mix of German, Lithuanian, Romanian. Even British girls fetch a pretty price."

"Why don't they run away instead of just standing there?" Brick asked.

"Because they'll be closely watched by a couple of the mafia's men sitting in a car somewhere. They run, they die, no second chances."

"What about the Russians?"

"They get too much money from them. They just

turn their backs on it all."

"Assholes."

"Yes."

They stopped outside the hotel. Brick made to climb out, but Grover stopped him with a hand on his arm. "Good luck."

"Yeah."

———————

The lobby of the Tatiana Hotel might be considered large, even huge by some standards. A highly polished terrazzo floor blanketed the space except for two squares of broadloom carpet that held some sofas, occasional tables and chairs A long mahogany bar was sited off to his right, with numerous barstools and a barman wearing a red vest.

Directly in front of him stood the doors to a glass elevator which serviced all four floors. The wall which housed the lift was of a peculiar design. Although appearing to be an external wall complete with windows, it was actually an interior one.

Brick ambled over to the reception counter, taking in his surroundings surreptitiously. The clerk looked up. "*Da ser? Chto ya mogu s•elat' •lya vas?*"

Brick said, "I'm sorry; I don't speak Russian."

"Tourist?" the man changed seamlessly to English with a smile.

"Something like that."

"What can I do for you?"

"I have a room booked. Wilson?"

"I will check."

The desk clerk tapped some keys on the keyboard and studied the screen before him. "Yes, Mister Wilson. Room …"

———————

Brick's room was large, as was the dark jacquard sofa against the wall next to the desk. A door led into a fully tiled bathroom, and the minibar fridge was fully stocked. The patterned carpet had been very recently cleaned, and the odor of sweet carpet shampoo still permeated the air.

Brick crossed to the bed where a large envelope, bulging at the seams, waited for him. He picked it up, opened it, and emptied the contents onto the dark coverlet. Typed words on crisp bond paper. He read it and dropped it back onto the coverlet. In several steps, he was at the end of the bed and proceeded to lift the mattress.

His actions revealed a suppressed handgun. Wedging his shoulder under the weight of the mattress, he bent and picked up the weapon, lowering and putting the bed to rights before unscrewing the suppressor. The weapon was an MP-443 Grach. Standard military issue for Russian soldiers.

Brick tucked it into his pants and placed the suppressor in his pocket. Then he crossed into the bathroom, opening the wall cabinet above the sink. He moved the complimentary shampoo and conditioner to one side, which revealed a set of car keys.

Scooping them up, Brick put them in his pants pocket, closed the cabinet, and walked back out into the main room. He found the television remote on a small table beside the sofa and pointed it toward the LED screen. With his finger on the power button, his action was interrupted by a slight noise. He froze. There was someone in the hallway outside his door.

Brick pressed the button, and the television flicked on. He adjusted the volume so that it could be heard from out in the hallway. With a flick of his wrist, he tossed it back onto the bed and hurried into the bathroom where he turned on the shower, hot water only.

The room quickly filled with steam; the mirror fogging up. Brick hid behind the door and waited.

Only seconds had passed before the bathroom door clicked open and began to swing on its hinges. The ex-SEAL held his breath, waiting for the intruder to move deeper into the room. But when whoever it was, hesitated, Brick didn't. He fired the Grach twice, the bullet punching through the bathroom door. The intruder dropped to the tiled floor and didn't move.

Brick kept the handgun up as he cautiously checked the body on his floor to make sure. He was much like the other one at the train station. Moving out into the main room to make sure that the man had been on his own, Brick crossed to the door to ensure the lock was engaged before returning to the body to see what he could discover. Definitely FSB, which meant there would be more and when their friend didn't show they would come.

He searched the dead man's pockets and found two things. A keycard and a picture of Richard Peters. "How the hell—"

Brick threw the card and put the picture in his pocket. Then he grabbed the dead man by the collar and dragged him all the way into the bathroom, trailing a red streak across the tiles. He dumped the corpse and turned the shower off, looking around before closing the door. Brick crossed back to the bed, gathering up everything he needed, then left the hotel, disappearing into the night.

London, Queens Birthday -1
MI5 Safehouse

By all external appearances, the MI5 safehouse looked like any other nondescript English Victorian double-story house. But the unassuming façade hid a hive of activity as the hunt for the Chechen terrorists continued.

Bruce Carey hit the end call symbol of his cell and turned to Thurston. "We've still got nothing. It's time to cancel all of the celebrations."

The general shook her head and stared at the suave looking man standing before her in his dark suit. "You can't. Doing that will tip the Chechens off that we know they are here, and they would detonate the device anyway."

The MI5 agent thought for a moment before saying, "There might be a way to at least save the royal family if this thing goes, how do you say it, tits up? We can use stand-ins."

"You have those?"

"Don't you people for your president?"

Thurston looked at him thoughtfully and said, "I don't really know. But it makes sense."

"Maybe you should if you don't."

"Maybe."

"Ma'am," Swift interrupted.

She turned to look at her tech. "What is it?"

"I might have something."

"Talk to me."

Swift brought his laptop over to them and touched a few keys. "I have been checking out airport arrival records for the past couple of days. Really the only way to get the package into the country in time. Or, so I thought. I also checked on all the smaller airfields around London but still came up with nothing. I then moved on to the Channel Tunnel and came across these which were captured yesterday."

A picture appeared of two people disembarking from the Eurostar in Kent. The photo was grainy, but there was a great deal of certainty as to their identity. Thurston said, "Tell me you know where they are."

"I lost them before they got to London," Swift explained. "But then I did some crosschecking with their known associates. Came up with nothing. But then I expanded the search and still came up with nothing. Then I got to thinking. Russian backed op."

"FSB safehouse?" Carey theorized.

"Yes. So, I did some hack – I mean looking around and came up with this."

Another picture appeared, this time of Barayev and Umarov entering a nondescript two-story building with the former carrying a smaller suitcase.

"That's them," Thurston said.

"Yes. It's somewhere near Hyde Park."

"I know where," Carey said. "We can be there in twenty minutes."

"Slick, get Kane and Cara. Tell them they've got a job to do. But they need to blend in. The rest of the team will gear up."

"Yes, ma'am."

Carey said, "I'll notify Hereford to have their special projects team put on standby just in case they are needed."

"Are they in London?"

"Yes. They're here for the festivities."

"OK, do it."

———————

London, Queen's Birthday -1

"Are we sure they're still even here?" Cara asked Kane.

"Slick hasn't seen them leave."

"Then what are we waiting for?"

"Confirmation, I guess."

"Shit," Cara cursed and climbed from the black Audi.

"Where are you going?"

"To get confirmation."

"Shit," Kane growled. "All units be aware, Reaper Two is approaching the target building."

"What's she up to, Reaper?" Ferrero asked over the comms.

"Going to see if anyone is home, Zero."

"Uh-huh. Reaper Four, do you have line of sight?"

"Copy, Zero, we got this," Axe replied. Beside him, he could hear the steady breathing of the SAS sniper. The SAS had arrived thirty minutes before and taken up position. "Reaper Two, just make sure you keep my firing line clear. Hate to have to shoot you in that pretty ass of yours."

"I am so going to kill you later, Axe," Cara joked.

"Not if I shoot you in the ass, ma'am."

"OK, I'm approaching the steps. Stand-by."

Kane watched her climb the concrete steps and then saw her knock.

He held his breath.

The door opened.

A man appeared. He frowned.

Kane heard Cara say, "Hello, sir. I seem to have lost my friends. Could you help me?"

"Go away."

She reached into her back pocket and took out the picture that they'd all been issued with featuring Barayev and Umarov. "Cara, what are you doing?"

She held up the picture with her left hand while her right was behind her back locked on the butt of her M17. "This is them."

The man moved suddenly, but Cara's hand flashed up, and she drove her handgun into his middle and squeezed the trigger. The muffled report sounded louder through the comms than out on the street. The man fell back, and Cara moved inside.

"Damn it!" Kane cursed. "Everyone move! Now!"

From a white van across the street, Brick and Arenas exploded from the back in full combat gear. With them were two SAS operators who would follow them in. Another team was covering the rear in case the occupants tried to squirt out that way.

Kane came out of the vehicle he and Cara had shared and started running across the street. The sound of more gunfire erupted from within the residence, only spurring Kane on.

Brick was the first to enter the doorway, hurdling the dead man Cara had shot first. Arenas was close behind him, and together they started past the stairs and into the lower half of the building. Behind them, the SAS men went up. No hesitation, just pure efficiency, carrying out their tasks like well-oiled machines. They were sometimes considered the best special operators in the world.

"Cara!" Kane called out as he entered the hallway.

"We're in here, Reaper!" Brick called out.

At the end of the hallway, a door opened out into a seventies-style kitchen, which was where he found his team. His hot gaze immediately locked on Cara. "That was a stupid fucking thing to do."

She shrugged. "It worked. We're in here."

A voice from one of the SAS operators on the second floor filled Kane's ear. "All clear up top, mate."

Kane looked at the man on the kitchen floor who moaned. "You shoot him?"

Cara shook her head. "Love tap."

"Where the hell are Barayev and Umarov?"

"Good question isn't it?" Cara said.

"Spread out, see what you can find."

As they each went their separate ways, Kane called it in. "Zero, they're not here."

"Say again, Reaper."

"They're not fucking here. Can't say it plainer than that."

"Roger that. Keep me updated."

"Roger. Out."

It was Arenas who located the shaft which had been dug in the basement. "Reaper, you better get down here."

Kane went downstairs into the cool concrete-lined room and found the Mexican standing over an open trapdoor. "I got us a tunnel."

"Damn it. They could have used it to get out at any time."

"There is someone who will know where they went."

"Yeah, the Russian."

"Reaper One, copy?"

It was Thurston. "Copy, Bravo."

"Your little fracas has drawn the attention of the Russian Ambassador who is claiming that safehouse as Russian territory. He's on his way down there now. This is going to kick up a shit storm of epic proportions."

"How long, ma'am?"

"Ten minutes."

"I'd best get started then."

"Started what?" Thurston asked.

"I have to question this guy we still have. The Chechens got out of here by using a tunnel that our friends the Russians dug under their sovereign territory."

"OK, do it. And don't stuff around."

Kane and Arenas hurried up the stairs. He called the SAS commander in and laid out the issue. The man nodded and said, "I'll put a couple of blokes on the front door. They'll keep him occupied."

"Thanks."

"What's happening?" a voice asked.

Kane looked at the doorway and saw Carey. "They got out through a tunnel. Coupled with the fact that the ambassador is on his way to declare war on us, things couldn't be better. The only way to find out what happened is to interrogate the bastard we have in the kitchen."

"Leave it to me, Old Chap. I've got this."

"Be my guest," Kane said.

When they walked back into the kitchen, they found the Russian FSB man had been tied to a chair. Carey looked at him and said, "I'm afraid, my good man, we don't have a lot of time. Let's make it quick and painless, shall we? Now, where did those dreadful Chechen terrorists go with their little package?"

"*Yebat' tebya!*" the Russian spat.

The handgun seemed to appear from nowhere. Just wasn't there and then it was, in Carey's fist. It crashed, and the bullet drove through the top of the FSB man's thigh, shattering bone as it went.

"Argh!" the man howled in pain.

"Try again, shall we?" Carey said. "Not got much time, remember? Where did they go?"

Pain. Deep, blinding, burning pain. Sweat broke out on the Russian's forehead and his teeth ground together. The muzzle of the handgun in the MI5 man's hand pressed against his good leg. "Any time now, old boy."

"Wait!"

"Yes?"

"They left a couple of hours ago."

"And went where?"

"That will be enough!" a loud voice came cutting across the kitchen.

The FSB man looked up at Kane and smiled. The ambassador had arrived.

"What is the meaning of this – this..."

Carey stared at the Russian ambassador for a moment before saying, "Just a bit of friendly chit-chat. Passing the time of day. Asking about the weather, what he's been up to, what his friends are going to do with their nuclear weapon? That kind of thing?"

"What?"

"You don't know? The FSB is working with some Chechen terrorists to smuggle a suitcase nuclear weapon into the country. Jolly bad sport if you ask me."

"Preposterous!"

"Not really. You see, it's already in London. And if we can't find it before it goes boom, we're all fucked."

The ambassador looked incredulous. "And you think Russia has something to do with it?"

"No," said Kane. "Just the FSB."

"Ridiculous. Now, get out of this building at once!"

"Can't do that," Kane told him. "We need that information."

"Sorry, old chap," Carey said to Kane. "I'm afraid we have to be gone."

"Shit."

The building was evacuated of all personnel, leaving only the Russian ambassador and his entourage. Once they were clear of the building, Kane asked Carey, "What the hell do we do now?"

"We keep going until we find the thing, or we're all dead."

CHAPTER NINETEEN

Moscow, Russia

The head of the Russian FSB's name was Luka Sobol. He was a career intelligence man who had come up through the ranks of the KGB back in the day and wasn't averse to the odd assassination plot when it was deemed necessary to be done. However, the reason for the bomb in Britain was solely due to their treatment of his Russia, deeming it inferior, second class. He would have preferred the three bombs, but alas, it wasn't to be so one would suffice. He felt the pain deep within his stomach bite. The cancer was playing up again. Its irritation was becoming both more frequent and severe, and he was acutely aware that it was only a matter of time now before it killed him.

He took a sip of the neat whiskey, felt it burn all the way down. Another glass or two and the pain would subside. Sobol reached out and picked up the two-thirds of a bottle and poured some more into the glass before replacing it onto the dark-stained wooden table. The orange glow of his lamp picked up the name on the dark label. Johnnie Walker Black.

It was his one vice that been acquired in his days as a KGB agent. His love of good whiskey. Shit, any whiskey.

Sobol picked up the television remote and turned the large LED screen on. China still had her troops amassed on the border with Kashmir. India and Pakistan were still fighting, although the peace talks looked as though there could be a ceasefire soon. Word had reached him about Melikov and his two men which meant they were getting close. But within twenty-four hours it would all be over. Twenty-four hours. That was all. Then it wouldn't matter.

Brick sat quietly in his vehicle, studying the building, watching for any movement, keeping tabs on lit and dark windows, taking his time before making a move. No point in rushing in there and winding up dead before he could achieve his mission. So, he continued to wait and watch.

Sobol had four bodyguards. Two outside and two in. Brick guessed that they were ex-Russian special forces. No doubt they would be armed. The stoop was lit, but the rest of the outside was now bathed in darkness.

It was time.

Brick reached into the back and retrieved a bottle of vodka from a paper bag. He unscrewed the lid and poured some of it onto his hand which he then used to splash about like cheap aftershave. Then he took a good pull and climbed out of the car.

Brick crossed the street in virtual darkness and once on the far sidewalk, began walking with an affected drunken stagger, mumbling incoherently. The closer he got to the Sobol's home, the louder he became. When he reached the house, he stopped, staggered a little more, and stared at the two men. He held up the vodka bottle and said, "Cheers, assholes."

One of the Russian bodyguards took a step forward and growled, "Fuck off drunk American."

Slurring: "Who the fuck you callin' drunk? I ain't drunk. Still kick yer Ivan ass."

The second bodyguard said something, and they both laughed. Brick's eyes narrowed. "The fuck you laughin' at?"

"Go away."

Brick placed the bottle on the sidewalk, pretending to check on it, whispering that he would be back for it, and stood up, taking a drunken step forward. "How about you make me, asshole."

The first bodyguard looked at his friend and shrugged. Then he started toward Brick, a smile still on his face. The confident grin disappeared, however, when he found himself staring at a fistful of suppressed Grach.

The weapon coughed, and the Russian lurched under the impact of the bullet. He fell forward at Brick's feet, missing the bagged bottle, shuddered, and then died. His friend reached instantly for his gun in a shoulder holster. He fumbled; never stood a chance. The Grach spat again, and by the orange glow cast by the stoop light, Brick saw a red patch appear on the man's shirt. The ex-SEAL shot them both again to make sure and then tried the door. It opened without a sound, so he stepped inside.

———

"What now?" Sobol asked the intruder.

Brick shrugged. "I kill you and leave, I guess."

The FSB man stared down at the body of his dead man on the floor near Brick's feet, still bleeding from the two holes in his chest. There was another in the doorway which led into his study. "I thought my men would have killed you before this."

"They tried."

Sobol shrugged. "It doesn't matter. It will all be over in a matter of hours, anyway."

"You seem mighty calm for a feller who's about to die," Brick observed.

"Now, later, it makes no difference. We all die. Some sooner than others."

"Not in their thousands like the atrocity you're

about to commit."

"The price of war. I do it for my country just as you are here to kill me for yours."

Brick shook his head. "This ain't for my country. This is just because you're a sadistic son of a bitch who is sanctioning state-sponsored terrorism."

"You would never understand, my friend."

"I ain't your friend. My only regret is that I can't kill you more than once."

"Regrets, we all have them. But, before you kill me, would you allow me just one more drink?"

Brick snorted. "Sure, why not? And while you're drinking tell me about your friend Melikov."

A smile split Sobol's lips. "How do you know we are friends?"

"Makes sense. Otherwise, you would have killed him a long time ago."

"His sister was my wife. Does that shock you?"

Brick said nothing, just watched the FSB man pour his drink, and take a sip before he continued. "I married her before the first time that Russian troops went into Chechnya. No one knew."

"What about all of the bombings?"

"What about them?"

"You knew he was responsible but did nothing about it."

"He was more useful alive than dead."

"So, while he killed hundreds of innocents, you looked the other way because he fed you intel?"

"Yes."

"What about this time? What changed?"

"There was no other way. He had to die before he had the chance to talk."

"Before he could tell us about the target of the nuclear attack?"

"Which you now know."

Brick said nothing. He didn't know, but he wasn't about to tell Sobol that. The Russian took another sip of his whiskey. "You should try this. It is good."

"How long have you been planning this nuclear attack?"

"Ever since we found out that that the Pakistani Ajeet Khan had stolen them. I used my network to find out the location of them and had Melikov use his people for the rest."

"Barayev and Umarov?"

"I think those were their names," Sobol said nonchalantly. He nodded at the television, the sound muted, the channel tuned to the pomp and ceremony of the celebrations underway for the Queen's birthday. "I was looking forward to watching it."

Brick glanced at it and saw a long shot of the twin rows of meticulously groomed men dressed in black and red, large bearskin hats upon their heads. Also, there were gun carriages drawn by six horses, a single rider on the offside front. A well-attended parade, a multitude of adoring fans watching on – "Son of a bitch."

Before Sobol recognized his mistake, Brick shot him through the forehead. The half glass of whiskey in the Russian's hand fell to the floor, the thick rug soaking up the liquid, the spilled contents leaving a dark stain.

As he walked toward the door, he removed the cell from his pocket, hitting the speed dial button for the number already embedded.

"Picca illy Cleaning."

"Gloria," Brick said and hung up.

He hurried through the front door onto the porch, stepping over the bodies as he went, and down onto the sidewalk. He walked swiftly across the street to the parked car, unlocking it, and pulling the lever for the gas tank. Then he screwed up a piece of paper into a long, thin taper which he placed halfway into the neck of the gas tank.

Brick reached back to his rear left pocket and found a book of matches he always carried. It was funny. Axe always carried a grenade; he carried a book of matches. He tore one off and struck it. The match flared to life, and he touched the orange flame to the tip of the paper. It quickly caught and began to burn.

Brick turned away from the vehicle and walked briskly along the darkened street. He hadn't gone far before it burst into flame, erasing all trace of his presence.

Thirty meters further on an Audi pulled up beside

him. Brick opened the door and climbed in. Grover was behind the wheel. "What's the emergency?"

"Horse Guards," Brick said to him. "The place where the bomb will be is Horse Guards."

———————

London, Queen's Birthday

"The Russian ambassador flew out of the UK an hour ago," Swift told Thurston.

"That rotten yellow son of a bitch," Thurston swore. "I guess he believes us now. Has MI5 been able to fix things up with the royal family?"

"It would appear that Her Majesty is a stubborn woman," Swift said. "I believe the words our friend from MI5 used were, "I was here through World War Two, and the trouble with the IRA. I'm too old to be running away now."

"So they didn't go?"

"Only the younger ones. She's going to be there today no matter what."

"Tough old broad."

"That she is ma'am."

"Well, then we'd best keep her alive. Do we have anything?"

Swift shook his head. "Trying to do this covertly is hard."

"And doing it overtly will just make them work faster. Keep trying."

Swift turned to leave when Ferrero appeared. "I just heard from our man in Moscow. Mission accomplished."

Thurston gave an abrupt nod of satisfaction. "Good."

"That's not all. We have a target. Horse Guards."

The general's eyes widened. "Shit, get the team together."

"Already in motion."

Horse Guards, London

Horse Guards was a place steeped in history. The new building had been built in the middle of the eighteenth century replacing the old one. Eventually, it had become an important headquarters. It was originally commissioned in the sixteen-hundreds, and now part of it was home to the Household Cavalry Museum.

Every year on the queen's birthday, an event was held on the large parade ground referred to as the trooping of the colors. A ceremony which dated back to the seventeen-hundreds to mark the official birthday of the British sovereign.

This day the queen would leave Buckingham Palace with an escort of Household Cavalry. Upon arriving at Horse Guards, she would inspect the troops on parade and then be escorted back to the palace.

The sun was out, and there were people already there eager for the parade to be underway. Above the Horse Guards building itself, the London Eye was visible across the Thames. Kane and Cara were dressed in civvies, just like the rest of the team. The SAS team was in position albeit out of sight around the parade ground and atop the building.

"Bravo Four, copy?"

"Loud and clear, Reaper."

"Do we have anything yet?"

"Like finding a needle in the proverbial English haystack," Swift came back to him.

Kane looked around the parade ground. "Where would you hide a suspicious-looking package around here? The way things are these days with terrorist scares, you'd think that it would have to be somewhere out of the way, quiet."

Cara nodded toward the Horse Guards building. "What about inside there?"

"Possible but far too obvious. Axe, take Carlos and go inside. They would only have access to the museum, which is open to the public. See if you can find anything."

"Copy."

Cara said, "If you were a wanted terrorist, and you knew your time was up, and there was a good chance that your plan was compromised, where would you go?"

"Here?"

Cara shook her head. "Here is where everyone is looking for you. Maybe a place where you can blend in, lots of people to mask your appearance."

"I take it that you have an idea?"

She smiled. "Bravo Four? Reaper Two."

"Go ahead."

"What is the closest tube station from our current position?"

"That would be Embankment Underground, Reaper Two."

Kane stared at her. "You figure that they're there somewhere?"

"As good a place as any. Slick, can you get into the security camera feed in there?"

"Give me a minute."

"Come on, Reaper. Let's go."

Kane spoke into his mic as he started to jog alongside Cara, "Bravo, Reaper One and two are moving."

"Where are you going, Reaper?"

"Embankment tube station."

"Why?"

"Cara has a hunch."

"It'd want to be a damned good hunch."

"Put it this way, ma'am," Cara joined the conversation. "If I'm wrong it won't matter much, will it? We won't be around to worry."

"Good luck."

Embankment Underground Station, London

Barayev and Umarov walked down the steps—against the flow of bodies rushing up and out onto the street—and onto the railway platform, the former carrying the case with the nuclear device. The last train pulled away from the station with a steady whine which slowly increased in pitch as it gathered speed. Halfway along the platform stood a security guard, his eyes roving over the throng of people, his gaze seeing but missing the two Chechens. They turned and walked along the platform in the opposite direction of the guard.

Suddenly, Barayev became aware of the fixed security camera directly ahead of them. He said to Umarov, "Keep your head down. Don't look up."

But it was too late. Those few grainy images captured by the camera were transmitted to a small laptop which sat in front of Sam Swift. "Gotcha."

"Reaper One, copy?"

"Copy."

"We've got them, Reaper. They've just landed in Embankment Station."

"Good work. Inform the general and get the SAS and bomb techs over there now. We're almost there. Don't lose them, whatever you do. This is the only chance we'll get."

CHAPTER TWENTY

Embankment Underground Station, London

Kane and Cara took the steps two at a time, descending into the bowels of the tube station until they reached the concourse at the bottom. It was almost clear now as the time for the parade was almost upon them and most people had arrived early to gain a good vantage point. The digital sign above the platform told them that the train from Wimbledon was still four minutes away.

"Slick, which way did they go?"

"You need to double back along the platform."

"Roger that," Kane replied and then saw the security guard. He hurried across to him and spoke urgently, "Listen carefully, you need to get all of these people out of here and seal the tube so no one can get down here."

The guard stared at him. "You're having a laugh

ain't you? Who the blooming heck are you, anyway?"

"I don't have time to explain. But believe me when I tell you that everyone down here is in danger. We're working with MI5."

"Listen, mate, the next train will be here in a couple of minutes. Most likely with a thousand people on it for the parade. Tell me how the fuck I'm going to stop them."

Kane knew he was right. "Just do what you can."

The Team Reaper commander turned away from him and said into his comms, "Bravo, copy?"

"Copy."

"We have to get this line shut down."

"I'll see what I can do."

Kane drew his M17 and walked past Cara, who was turned in the opposite direction. "Shall we?"

"Why not?"

"Slick, where are they?"

"They entered the tunnel up ahead of you."

"Christ, that's all we wanted. Like a fucking episode of Jack Bauer."

"Who?" Slick asked.

"Never mind."

Kane and Cara reached the end of the platform and were about to step down when he remembered something. "Wait. The next train will be here in a moment."

"We haven't –"

A two-toned chiming noise rang out throughout

the underground, preceding an automated message announcing the arrival of the next train before Cara even finished her sentence. It slid gracefully from the tunnel and slowed to a stop leaving sufficient room for the two of them to climb down onto the tracks.

"Let's not touch the rails," Cara advised. "We'll light up like a darn Christmas tree if we do."

Behind them, the doors of the carriages opened, burgeoning a flood of humanity from within its crowded compartments, the associated noise flowing on the tide; laughter, happiness, loud voices, whistles, cell phone rings, filtering along the platform.

"Slick, you still got us?"

"Loud and clear, Reaper."

"Have you got them at all?"

"Wonderful thing the London tube system. Cameras all the way along it. Not many people know about it. Long story short, yes, I have them. I have you too. Ahead of you about a hundred meters is a service tunnel. It branches away to your left. It looks like it goes into a large storage room of some kind. You might need to hurry as they look like they're getting it set up."

"What effects could the weapon have, being det-onated underground, Slick?" Cara asked. "Don't they test these things underground?"

"In a contained environment. This won't stop much at all."

Kane and Cara moved faster, jogging along the

rocky berm beside the track until they reached the mouth of the service tunnel. "Um, guys," Swift said, "they just hugged. Shit, shit, shit."

"So what?" Kane said.

"He means they were saying goodbye."

"Oh. That's not good."

"No."

They made their way along the service tunnel until they reached the door to the storage room. Surprised that it wasn't kept under lock and key, Kane eased the door open and was faced with row upon row of steel shelves piled with equipment. They slipped inside, using hand signals to indicate which way they would go, and split up. In their comms, Swift said, "They know you're there."

Even though Kane knew they were there and expecting him, he was still surprised when Barayev appeared in front of him. It was only pure reflex that saved his life. The first bullet whistled past his nose and punched into a box on one of the shelves. Kane's M17 spat back, but he missed by a good way. The pair began trading lead, and while they did, Cara tried to circle around them for a shot at the shooter.

In doing so, however, she was momentarily distracted and was blindsided by Madina Umarov.

The Chechen woman hit Cara with a shoulder, causing her to lose her grip on her weapon. It skittered across the concrete floor and under a stack of shelves. The pair hit the floor hard, and for a moment

Cara was stunned.

Umarov rolled on top of her and hit her twice in the face, sending blood flooding into Cara's mouth. Stars flashed brightly before her eyes, and in the distance, she could still hear Kane and Barayev exchanging gunfire.

Regaining control of her senses, Cara bunched her muscles and arched her back. Then she rolled, throwing Umarov to the side. "Get off me, you fucking bitch!"

The Chechen woman was flung sideways with a loud yelp. She crashed against a row of shelves with an impressive grunt. Cara swept to her feet just in time to meet another charge from Umarov. The bitch was like a cat. She came in hard, and Cara's right fist shot forward, flattening her nose against her face, stopping her in her tracks.

Umarov staggered back, her hands up to her bleeding face. Cara stepped in close and hit her again, this time with the heel of her right hand between her breasts. It was a savage blow that caused the woman to gasp for breath.

Spitting blood, Cara went after Umarov, wanting to keep the ascendency. In desperation, the Chechen spun on her right heel and brought her left foot up in a vicious arc which, had it connected, would have more than likely broken Cara's jaw.

Instead, the glancing blow was enough to unbalance Cara, and she cannoned into a sturdy steel shelf which seemed to bite into her ribs. She turned back to face Umarov who hit her flush on the jaw. She shook her head and tried again.

This time the Chechen hit her just above the left eye, opening the flesh on her brow which began to bleed profusely, blinding her on one side.

In the background, more shots could be heard, and Cara thought, *I hope he's *oing better than me.*

Clearing her vision with a quick wipe, the blood continued to run down the side of Cara's face, dripping onto her shirt in a deep red stain. Umarov smiled at her, revealing pink teeth stained with blood from her nose. "I kill you now, bitch."

Cara spat blood once more and snarled, "Bring it!"

Umarov lowered her head and charged. Her shoulder caught Cara in the middle, and she was certain that she felt a rib give way under the crunching blow. She was propelled backward and once more was smashed into the steel shelves. Grinding her teeth against the pain of it all, Cara brought down her clasped hands in one large fist. The blow crashed down on Umarov's back and drove her down to her knees. As the Chechen went down, Cara brought up her right knee, catching the woman under the chin.

Umarov's head snapped back, and her eyes grew glazed. She seemed to teeter on the edge for a moment lingering in a semi-conscious state. Blowing hard, Cara grabbed a handful of hair and raised the woman's head. "You've got this coming, bitch."

Cara's fist drove into Umarov's face and tipped her over the edge into oblivion. "Bravo, Tango Two is down, over."

"Copy. Get to that bomb."

Kane could feel the blood running down his left arm, dripping from the end of his fingers. There was a wet patch of blood on his right side as well, a deep burning pain emanating from torn flesh. Both injuries were caused by ricochets and weren't life-threatening, but they hurt like a bitch.

Barayev fired again, the bullet howling off the side of a stack of shelves. Kane leaned out and blew off three rounds at the Chechen. He saw the man's leg kick out as a bullet drilled into it, bringing forth a howl of pain. Kane went to fire again, but the M17 was empty. He loaded in a new magazine and racked home a fresh round.

"Give it up, Barayev. It's over," Kane called out.

"It will be shortly. There is nothing you can do to stop it."

"Don't be so sure about that."

"Who will stop it? You?" he sneered.

"Just as soon as I can." Kane's last words were greeted by silence.

"Cara, where are you?"

"Not far away," she whispered from behind him. She frowned when she noticed that he was bleeding.

"Are you OK?"

"Just a scratch. You?"

"Same."

"Where's Umarov?"

Cara snorted derisively. "That bitch. She's having a nap."

"We're running out of time; we have to stop him now and get to that nuke."

Cara took a deep breath and was about to move when Kane stopped her. "No. My turn this time."

Kane stepped out from behind the row of shelves and started forward. His M17 was raised at shoulder level, and he was squeezing off steady shots. Barayev fired back, several slugs displacing the air close to Kane. The Team Reaper commander fired three more rounds which forced the terrorist back into cover.

He didn't stay there long though, and appeared once more, this time with a crazed expression on his face. It twisted into a snarl, and he opened his mouth to scream something when a bullet punched into his ugly maw, shattering teeth and blowing through his spine as it exited. He dropped like a marionette with its strings cut, dying there on the dirt-covered floor.

"Clear!" Kane called out with relief. "Bravo, Tango One is down."

"Copy, Reaper One. Now find that bomb!"

Kane and Cara found the suitcase nuke less than a minute later. The lid was down, and they hesitated briefly before Cara said, "Can't stop it if we don't open the damned thing."

"You want to do the honors?"

"If you mean killing us, why not?"

She stepped forward and flicked the two latches. The sound made by the metal catches was almost deafening as she expected the act to kickstart some cataclysmic event. But nothing happened. Next, she lifted the lid and there it was. It looked so small for something which could have such massive repercussions. Cara looked at the digital display, which was steadily counting backward to doomsday. She turned her head and said with a wry smile, "We've got thirty seconds."

Kane couldn't believe what he had just heard. "Bravo, did you get that last transmission?"

"Copy, Reaper One."

"Fuck!" Kane shouted at the top of his voice. Veins popped in his neck as his anger released.

Cara looked at the timer.

00:25...

"I'm sorry, Reaper," she said in a quiet voice.

"What for?"

She shrugged. "I just am."

00:20...

"Me too," he said and walked over to her. He knelt and put his arm around her shoulders.

00:15...

"Do you think somebody will know?"

"Know what?"

"What we've done."

00:10...

He squeezed her shoulder. "Yeah, they'll know."

"It's funny; I thought I'd be scared."

00:05...

"Yeah."

00:03...

"Bye, Reaper."

"Bye, Cara."

00:01...

They closed their eyes, prepared to be blown to kingdom come.

Nothing happened.

Five seconds went by; ten. Kane and Cara opened their eyes and looked down at the clock.

00:00...

Epilogue

"How are you two feeling?" Thurston asked as she entered the rehab room.

Kane and Cara looked at her. "Like I've been shot … twice."

"Ribs are still busted, ma'am. The eye will heal."

She gave them a warm smile. "Could have been worse."

Which was true. The bomb techs did explain what had gone wrong with the device, but the pair couldn't remember the technical term that was used. Something to do with a malfunction of the flux capacitor or some such bullshit…maybe that was the movie Back to The Future. They didn't understand. They were alive, and so were thousands of others. None of them realized just how close they had come to dying in the blink of an eye.

"Is Brick back yet?" Kane asked.

"Tonight."

"Any word on Traynor?" Cara inquired.

"He's back in the States. So is Teller."

"What news of the Russians?"

Thurston nodded. "Not a word. Brick sent us an audio file he recorded on a cell he had while he was with Sobol. The CIA has it and are intending to use it if they decide to kick up a stink. Who would have guessed that he and Melikov were brothers-in-law?"

Kane's eyebrows shot up. "Really?"

"Really."

There was movement in the doorway, and Carey entered the room. "You pair look like rundown crumpets."

"A what?" Cara asked.

"Never mind. How are you feeling?"

"Like Crumpets."

Carey chuckled. "Feel like a visitor? There's someone out there that wants to see you."

"Tell them to come back next week," Kane growled.

"Oh, come on, old boy. You'll want to see this one."

"Shit, all right. Make it quick, though."

Carey disappeared for a moment and then returned. He stood beside the doorway, and a short, elderly woman wearing a yellow dress and small yellow hat entered, followed by two men in suits. She shuffled across the room to where Kane and Cara stood with confused expressions on their faces. Off to the left, Thurston stood at attention.

The new arrival stopped and stared at Kane, smiled warmly, and said, "Hello."

Kane's jaw dropped. "Oh shit."

If you Liked Empty Quiver, you might enjoy The Termination Protocol (Scott Stiletto Book 1)

The Termination Protocol is the first book in the hard-edged, action thriller series – Scott Stiletto.

The United States is under siege, and the enemy has help from the White House!

Scott Stiletto is one of the CIA's toughest assets, a veteran of numerous missions, an operative with compassion and ruthlessness in equal parts.

His enemy is the New World Revolutionary Front, a terrorist organization seeking to overthrow the government of the United States and install their own puppet--a willing puppet, who is already very close to the president he wishes to replace.

With freedom and justice hanging in the balance, Scott Stiletto gives no quarter. He will give the enemy a one-way ticket to hell!

"...99% pure action fun, no additives. I had to stop reading the book several times just to catch my breath..."

AVAILABLE NOW

ABOUT THE AUTHOR

A relative newcomer to the world of writing, Brent Towns self-published his first book, a western, in 2015. Last Stand in Sanctuary took him two years to write. His first hardcover book, a Black Horse Western, was published the following year. Since then, he has written a further 26 western stories, including some in collaboration with British western author, Ben Bridges.

Also, he has written the novelization to the upcoming 2019 movie from One-Eyed Horse Productions, titled, Bill Tilghman and the Outlaws. Not bad for an Australian author, he thinks.

He says, "The obvious next step for me was to venture into the world of men's action/adventure/thriller stories. Thus, Team Reaper was born."

A country town in Queensland, Australia, is where Brent lives with his wife and son.

For more information:
https://wolfpackpublishing.com/brent-towns/

Made in the USA
Las Vegas, NV
24 April 2021